THE COLLECTORS

by

Jorge Sastre

and

H.A.L. Wagner

PUBLISHED BY

Forker Media
1450 SOM Center Rd, Suite 23
Mayfield Heights, OH 44024
www.forkermedia.com

THE COLLECTORS © 2012 JORGE SASTRE, H.A.L. WAGNER
ISBN: 978-0-9883972-2-4

About the Authors:

JORGE SASTRE was born in Montevideo, Uruguay, he is a long time resident of Florida, USA. He now resides in Daytona Beach, Florida, with girlfriend Ellen. He debuted as a professional wrestler in 1996 and later became a trainer at the I.W.S independent wrestling school. In his spare time, he enjoys wrestling, soccer, photography and writing.

H.A.L. WAGNER grew up a Navy Brat and lived on both coasts seeing many different cultures. He received his B.A. in History from the University of Florida. He currently resides in Richmond, VA with his wife, Natasha and dog, Charlie, but Florida will always be home.

….Dedicated to that Number 4 dog and all the gamblers that bet on him...

Prologue

LESTER walked out of Spanky's Games and Laundry feeling good. He was up fifty grand and wearing a pair of clean briefs. The Atlantic Ocean pushed damp salty air over land, tossing Lester's comb-over out of place. Everything was going his way, too bad he did not pay his debts on time.

Tucked between the reaches of two parking lot lamps sat Luis and John Solo. Two days ago Boss Logan Ducci phoned the brothers that Lester had been dodging lower rung collectors and evaded all previous attempts for repayment. With a good network of underworld informants the brothers caught up to Lester on this hot summer night. The brothers waited in Luis' car for the borrower to leave.

Luis cranked the engine and the car roared to life. He flipped on the head lamps and crawled the car from the parking space. Crawling forward, the brothers neared Lester as he walked to his own car.

Lester snapped a look over his shoulder, quickening his pace as the pearl sedan slithered under the parking lights. Suddenly the engine growled and leapt past Lester. Luis cut the wheel and the car separated the debtor from his ride outside of Spanky's.

The driver's door opened first. A fine pair of Italian leather shoes touched down on the coquina infused asphalt. From the passenger's side came a pair of scuffed black leather jump boots. The doors to the pearl Cadillac were left open, this would not take long.

"Oh hey Luis, John." Lester forced a grin to separate his lips. "I didn't recognize you there for a...a..." Lester let his words fade. He knew why two of the best collectors to work East Town were standing in a parking lot at one a.m.

"So Lester, how have the tables been treating you?" Luis stood beside his car with folded arms. John moved to Lester's left. John and Luis were positioned far enough apart that Lester could not look at the pair without turning his head.

"I've stayed away from all that. I'm keeping clean." Lester could not help but look back at the gambling going on through the window of the laundromat.

"Then how do you expect to pay back your loan?"

"You know I'm good for it Luis, I swear. I told Ducci I'd have it by the end of the month."

"You need to pay us something now, to show a little good faith Lester." John removed his hands from his pants pocket.

Lester felt the soles of his cheap shoes scrape backwards against the coquina asphalt as his armpits moistened and sweat rolled down the center of his back. "C'mon John. How long we go back? Look, tell Ducci…"

Luis threw a shot to Lester's gut. The man gasped and dropped to one knee. Luis' expensive shoe landed on Lester's back. Lester's face melted into the asphalt. John leaned down and pulled Lester to his feet. The pair of collectors had been at this game for a few years now. Together they had developed multiple tools to make each collection as simple as possible so they could go back to the same tables where these gambling junkies had lost everything. John and Luis loved to gamble just as much as the men they collected on.

Their system was not good cop bad cop - there were no cops. "We went to bat for you, Lester. Ducci wanted you dead and we got an extension on your life. How are you going to pay your loan if you're dead?"

Lester caught his breath and said, "Yeah, yeah I can't pay nothing if I'm dead. I was just aahh… I was trying out a new system." Lester reached into his coat pocket. The Brothers both drew pistols. Lester dropped a stack of Playing Chips, the currency of a gambling addicted town.

"Whoa, hey! Take it easy." Lester went down on his knees with his hands raised. As he gathered up the chips he said, "I've got most of it here. I swear I can get the rest in a week. Just give me another week." He reached up and handed what he gathered to John.

"What is this" John said thumbing through the stack. "Forty, fifty grand? " John handed the red and black chips off to the other collector.

Lester got to his feet and dusted off his hands and knees. "That squares us for now right? Tell Ducci-"

John interjected, "You're late on a payment and we find you with half the debt and that makes us square. What do you think Ducci will say if we let you go without a beating."

"Can't you just tell him..." The Collectors stopped listening. John launched a nasty right across Lester's cheek. Lester went down swiftly. Luis and John stomped Lester for a while. As the beating got underway, Playing Chips fly. Like a heavy rain, the chips hit the ground spinning and rolling. A debt was collected and another junkie learned a lesson, Boss Ducci style.

****

This is the life in East Town Florida. Years ago this was a quiet little beachside town, letting the Atlantic lap at its white sandy beaches, sustaining on seasonal tourist dollars. Tourism was finicky leaving too many peaks and valleys in resident's wallets. The majority of the year round residents were blue haired retirees with sketchy grown children who could not quite make it on their own. They were the wrong kind of boomerang kids, the kind that came back after prison or to steal a couple of wrinkled twenties from grandma to get a fix.

Every generation would come into their own in this sleepy beach town. Each one had grandiose dreams of making the place world famous, but at what cost. There was the auto race track bringing in fans with thirty foot RVs and money to spend. That was twice a year. Then came the bikers. At first on their own in gangs then the doctors and lawyers joined them and that was twice a year. College kids found their way there every year starting with sheet white Canadians in late February. They were easy to spot: socks stuffed into flip-flops and wearing shorts and tank tops while the locals wore parkas. No amount of tourism dollars was enough to satisfy the town councils coffers.

These attempts to attract people to town created a few winners but too many losers. The people wanted more. They wanted something that would last, they got it the day the one armed bandit came to town.

Hotels could not convert banquet halls into gaming rooms fast enough. The little mom and pop ten room motels were torn down as twenty story concrete high rises lined the beachside blocking the sun from the mainland. Slot machines covered every wall and a variety of gaming tables filled the center. Soon gas stations put up video poker and doctors' offices opened up off track betting while you wait.

Gambling took hold turning everyone and everything sick. It was a virus, spreading through every facet of life in East Town from the deadbeat street walkers to the mansion dwelling millionaire. The rising tide lifted all boats and even sent a few into dry dock. Cash became scarce. The economy in this beach town began to change. Starting with people dealing strictly in cash like drug dealers and prostitutes, switched to multi colored playing chips became valid substitutes for greenbacks. A new currency began on the streets as gambling junkies began trading in casino chips for goods they did not have the cash for. Soon convenient stores began accepting chips for beer and cigarettes.

Banks could not handle the requests for loans and credit card advances. Pawnshops where over stocked with more gold and diamonds than they could hold, problem was no one wanted it. The price of gold might have been climbing elsewhere in the world but in East Town, it might as well have been tin. With pawn shops no longer able to give out cash the people turned to sharks. Loan Sharking became an accepted form of banking with interest rates fluctuating like that of any other lending institution. These loans had much greater consequences if they were not paid on time.

If a loan shark could not get his money back from a fish then he couldn't stay in business. In order to ensure a return, a loan shark hired a collector. This is the story of two of the best collectors to ever work East Town.

John Dunn and Luis Rodriguez did not start off as brothers, not in the sense as most. They did not share blood by any means, no mother or father or even step parents that would tie them together. These two boys grew up in the foster program of East Town. Like most of the kids in the home, they were left by junkie parents who would rather spend four dollars on the slots then on breakfast for their child.

Somewhere around age twelve, though neither one knew their actual birthdays, John and Luis met. For several years after that, they managed to stay together in and out of multiple homes. It was a dog eat dog world in most of the homes. Foster parents filing their houses with kids to collect a government check that went right to the casinos. Without any other stable family life, John and Luis decided they would become brothers.

Luis turned eighteen first and stuck around East Town until John was free from the foster program. Knowing that they would never lead a good life in East Town, they left, hoping to build a life elsewhere. They packed up their stuff, changed their names to respect the bond they had forged, said goodbye to their crap jobs the social worker set up for them and drove out into the desert.

It was one dusty town after the next for the new brothers John and Luis Solo, with each as bad as the last. Minimum wage jobs came and went. The brothers searched for legitimate work but it did not come easy. There was the gig as bouncers, the time on the independent wrestling circuit and the occasional security detail. Every time things started to look promising, someone had a temper flare up and it was time to move on. It was always a boss who pushed his authority too far or a customer who did not know when to shut the hell up.

Things on the road were not working for the brothers. A call from a guy they knew while in the foster program let the brothers know there were jobs with a hotel and it wasn't bad. With no other recourse or money the two moved home.

****

Over oxygenated air pumped out at sixty-eight degrees from vents high in the casino ceiling. Laser lights pointed up from the corners of the room projecting soft changing lights across the ceiling. Flashing lights were everywhere luring people to drop a coin in them. Along the floor, two casino guards pushed money around in a locked metal cart. One side was filled with cash and the other balanced out with coins. The cart left a pair of one inch wide trenches in the plush paisley carpet.

"I hate hauling this shit around." Luis said tugging on the collar of the maroon and grey polyester guard's uniform. "I thought we came back to this town to make money not push it around all day. There's got to be something else, anything."

John exhaled all he had, "I hear ya brother. We tried living out there in the real world but life in East Town is well..." John looked at a group of scantily clad show girls walking by. Through a headdress of feathers one gave John a smile. "It's not too terrible." John continued, "But don't sweat it, look around at all these fat cats cashing in. Our numbers will hit soon. Just think of this job as a momentary chore, a quick little side job until we find what it is we really want."

Luis was quick on his rebuttal, "I just don't want to end up like Frank over there." He had spotted Frank which spawned the conversation. The guard had grey hair and a pot belly he passed off as a barrel chest. Frank had a handkerchief out blotting away the perspiration on his brow. He had been warned about sweating too much on the job, how it was bad for appearances.

It was not far for the brothers to go with the cart. The pair stopped at a locked door. John swiped a security card and both men were prompted to lean in for retinal scans. Security was tight around the casino. This particular room held the tightest security of all. It was the vault. The door and the scanner were just the first part in an elaborate system of hallways and locked doors leading to the counting room. The brothers took an elevator down below the casino where they were x-rayed then a combination hand print and voice recognition verification eventually opened the vault door.

Once inside they signed over the cart so that some fellow low wage earner could count the million or so dollars flowing into the casino on an hourly basis. The brothers did not care any longer; their shift had come to an end. It was time to clock out and hit the dog track or see if any of their friends were playing Jai Alai today.

John stretched a cord of plastic security keys from his belt and thumbed to the one that would unlock the guard's station. Luis tapped him on the shoulder and pointed without saying a word. From a low lit corner of the casino two men struggled. Feeling a sense of duty, and being justice minded men, the pair made their way across the casino floor.

The man who started the commotion was large in proportion with a salt and pepper head that protruded without a neck from broad shoulders. With one arm he held a gangly man by the neck against the wall. The smaller man flailed spindly arms and legs like a crushed insect who did not know he was dead yet.

The guards shouted for the large man to let go. The bulky attacker refused to comply. The brothers grabbed hold and began to shake the older man as if an apple would drop from above. It only took a second of broken concentration on the old man's part to allow the nearly dead insect a chance to escape. The man broke free and ran out the nearest exit.

"You mutha fu...mutha fu.." The old guy struggled to regain his breath. "You two idiots cost me one hundred and twenty grand." He reached for his back pocket. The brothers pulled their cattle prods (as they were not authorized to carry guns). The bulky man produced a white handkerchief and wiped at his forehead.

Luis started the interrogation, "What the hell do you think you're doing robbing a guy in *our* casino?"

"That shit bag owed me money and I was collectin'." Ducci leaned his sequoia shaped trunk against the wall.

"So you're a loan shark." The brothers had never seen a Loan Shark around the hotel before. Most deals were conducted over the phone like civilized people. Occasionally a collector would make an appearance and escort the gambler out of the hotel. It never got messy on a casino floor.

"Damn right." Ducci remarked with reassuring confidence. "The best in town kid. See, if a Shark can't get his money from a fish, then he ain't in business no more." Ducci laid off holding the wall up. His voice grew an octave, "And soon the other sharks eat him alive. That bastard has been run'n all over town playn' wit my money and I finally had him." Out of breath a second time he resumed his position against the wall.

From the center of the casino floor a well dressed man with tanned leather for a face glad handed the few Q-tip old ladies that had taken a bus from

Sarasota to gamble at the Fabulous Beach Palm. His smile was bright and his eyes kind as he cupped each of the old bag's hands, thanking them for their journey. Despite the political scene, he kept an eye on the two guards and the large man in the corner. Behind this distinguished elder, was a man six and a half feet tall clad in all black with a cord from an earpiece running down his neck.

The old man spoke, "Gentlemen, this is the main gaming floor. Commotion like this is reserved for outside or a back alley." The kindness in his eyes was gone as he looked his two security guards up and down. The old man was Sam Dennis, seventy three year old owner of the Fabulous Beach Palm Casino and Hotel. His suit was cut sharp and tight wrapping a light grey mesh pattern around his body. It was the suit of a man one quarter his age. No doubt picked out by his current wife and all her twenty one years of life. "Now what seems to be the trouble here?"

The three remained quiet like schoolchildren on the playground busted for rough housing.

"Well..." Sam folded his arms.

Ducci grumbled then coughed up, "These two fuck-ups fucked up. I had me a fish and some real dough coming my way."

"Luis...John is this true?"

"Yes sir. We ended their struggle." Luis said believing they had done nothing wrong.

Sam turned his attention back to Ducci, "So Mister." He paused, "This is where you fill in your name."

"Names Ducci, Boss Ducci. I run Pawn Sharks over off State Street." The Boss said heaving up his trousers.

"I'm sure. Anyway I take it you are a loan shark with all the proper billing and collecting I.D.'s per this wonderful state?" This was nothing new to Sam Dennis. Working with loan sharks, no matter how detestable was the norm. Fact was the Sharks kept guys coming into casinos.

Ducci nodded. He had to keep his cool if he was ever going to loan money around the Fabulous Beach Palm. He reached into his rear pocket and produced a small brass badge of an eagle with wings spread over a shield. Inscribed on it were the words "Registered Loan Shark" and under that "Collector". The photo in the ID matched with the man and the badge looked real enough. The serial number on the bottom of the badge could be checked but Sam was convinced of its authenticity. Ducci was a registered Loan Shark and Collector with the state of Florida.

Sam nodded his approval. "My two honest employees here fouled up a recovery for you. Well, my young guards will make amends I am sure of it. But next time Boss, give my security detail the heads up if you plan on collecting in my casino." Sam gave everyone that movie star smile and proceeded back through the casino floor.

Sam flashed that politician grin to his employees then walked off.

"Mr. aahh...We feel really bad about..."

"The name's Boss Ducci, ya douche bags." John and Luis stared unimpressed. The title of Boss did not have the effect Ducci had hoped. To some the name may strike fear but the brothers are still naive to the major players in the East Town underworld. They have yet to view the savagery Boss Ducci is capable of dealing.

"Don't worry Boss Ducci, my brother and I will get your money back." John confessed.

"Yeah well, hold up, brothers? You don't look like no friggin' brothers. This ones brown like a, a..." Logan jerked a thumb towards Luis and leaned in as if to tell a racist joke.

John came back with a pointed finger at Ducci and said through a clenched jaw, "Choose your next words carefully old man." The decision of a white kid to become brothers with a brown kid was sure to confuse people regardless if they were in a country club or a barrio. The brothers had to face all sorts of insults, usually about their mother getting around, but they did not sweat it. Their real parents were dead to them so who cared if a fictitious mother was a slut, for all either one of them knew it was true.

Ducci untwisted his face as he began to laugh at these two young and dumb "brothers". They really showed brass balls even if they were tucked in the guard's polyester trousers. Something about the way the pair interacted as one impressed the rising crime boss.

Ducci pulled out a scratch pad with notes on it. He handed it to Luis, who scanned it then passed it along to John. In scribbled short hand were notes on Juan Gomez's movements and habits. Nothing stood out as a solid lead.

"This is all I have on that bastard." Ducci growled. "You find him you get five percent. You find him and think of crossin' me, the last thing you see is a muzzle flash." Ducci made like a gun with a forefinger and thumb. He pointed the gun at the brothers and dropped the thumb hammer on the finger pistol. The brothers put on tough faces with a "can-do" attitude attached knowing inside failure would not be an option.

As the brothers walked off, Ducci called after them, "Hey hold up. You guys'll need some badges."

John ripped a smile across his face. Luis shook his head "no" for his brother to keep his mouth shut, this was no time to be a comic.

"I ain't kidin' around. If the Law sees you collecting without one you're sunk. Take mine. I'll vouch for ya if you screw up, but don't screw up." Ducci pointed his finger gun once more. Despite Ducci's tired eyes and white hair the brothers knew Ducci had it in him to make good on that threat.

The brothers put the word out for Juan Gomez through their own channels. A tip came in from a friend of theirs, Beltran (a Jai Alai player) that the man they were looking for was still in town staying at the Sundowner over on the mainland. Beltran was usually good for tips on which Jai Alai player was about to be deported, that was the guy you bet on. Tonight he offered up something on Gomez, the skinny indebt gambler.

Off US 1, away from the beachside and its pulsing neon lights, the Sundowner Motel was normal for the mainland part of town. A couple of drug deals and a hooker came and went. A homeless man pushed a shopping cart full of dumpster prizes for the day. The brothers watched as guests signed in and out for the last two hours. Judging by the hourly turnover, the Sun Downer was a favorite for prostitutes and druggies looking for a place to trick or trip. With a client list such as it was, the manager knew not to rat out a guest. Asking him for information would spook any number of fish hiding out in the dump. They had to be sure Juan was there.

Luis swung his black Nissan past the motel once then backed into a spot across the street. Inside the glow of an LED smart phone illuminated the interior. An announcer's voice, high and nasally, emitted from the little speaker in the top of the phone. "Here comes Unlucky. And they're off."

John held the phone streaming simulcast dog racing close to his face. "Damn the four dog got bumped!" John slapped the dash with the race form.

"Let me see that program again." Luis reached out as John handed him the racing form they picked up earlier. He scribbled numbers in the margins while performing rudimentary math. The words he mumbled came out in Spanish.

"Next race let's put the four six wheeled with the five seven eight."

John punched numbers on the face of the phone. He looked to Luis, "You sure?"

Luis nodded.

"Done." John hit send and their wager went through.

With six minutes to post time, there was nothing to do but watch the motel. A second prostitute had come and gone from room six. This particular prostitute was taller than the others, squared at the hips and bowed at the legs. The brothers got out of the car and headed for the room. It was time to move.

Luis rapped on the two-inch thick glass of the motel manager's window. The sign above read *Customer Service* - he doubted the truth behind it. The manager came from around a corner. He was stout, in need of a shave and clad in nothing but a soiled brown robe. He flipped a switch and a scratchy voice came out of a screened cylinder in the glass, "It'll be twenty-five an hour or fifty for the whole night, plus a linens charge."

"We're looking for Juan Gomez, heard he was here."

"Sorry fellas, client patient confidentiality." The manager used his middle finger to push up on thick lenses wrapped in thin metal frames.

Luis slapped the glass. The manager did not flinch, but instead smiled. John dug into his pocket and flashed the collections badge Ducci had given him. Tapping it against the glass, he smiled back.

The manager's smile faded. He believed he ran a quiet establishment that catered to local clientele, such as the streetwalkers and tramps slumming up and down this stretch of US 1. People who skip on Sharks don't make very good clients. But that's why it is a cash up front business.

"Piss off collectors. This is private property." The manager knew the law, private property only kept collectors out until they had a visual on their collection. Then they could come and go as they pleased. Green to the business, the brothers backed down from the manager's legal threat.

Back in the car parked across the street the brothers sat. Luis looked up from a well-marked and notated racing form to watch another messy haired androgynous hooker leave from room twenty-six in the last two hours. Luis muttered something about two hookers in two hours from room twenty-six but John was too engrossed in the five-card stud app on his phone. He was in the middle of a bluff when Luis repeated himself. John went all in.

"Okay brother, let's go find out if he's in there." John said finally looking up from his phone.

The two got out of the car and walked toward the door of room 26.

"Twenty says we get him here and now." Luis flipped a poker chip into the air, opened his shirt pocket and together they watched it drop.

"You're on."

At the door of room twenty-six, John leaned back to kick open the door. Luis stopped him. He knocked softly. The door opened.

The fish was standing in tighty-whities badly in need of washing. His jaw sunk into his neck as Luis pushed him into the room. John followed quickly grabbing the fish then tossing him to the floor. The man let out a shout that was cut short by a blow to the kidney from John who was on top of the gambler.

"You stupid son of a bitch, you just cost me twenty." John ground his knee into the man's back. A muffled whimpered sank into the musty shag carpet. John held Gomez's left arm bent unnaturally behind his back.

Luis checked out the rest of the small single bed motel room. Coming out of the bathroom, he let John know the place was empty.

The fish on the floor regained his breath. He tried to look up but could only see Luis' shoes move across the floor headed for the bag. It was a familiar bag to Luis, the kind casinos give out to winners.

"Is this some kind of robbery?" His eyes strained in the corners of their sockets. "Hey, I know you from the Beach Palm." He said looking up at John. John twisted a knee forcing out a groan from the skinny naked man. "Okay, okay my mistake. Are you robbing me?"

"We're Collectors and its time you paid up in full." John shoved a badge into the man's face.

Luis stood with his foot inches from Gomez's rug burned face. "How much is this?"

Gomez remained quiet. If they were real Collectors, they would take it all and if they were robbers, they would take it all.

John's knee twisted in the gambler's back. The gambler winced again.

Pain forced the words as he said, "About ninety-five G's! Just take it and go! Please!" Gomez groaned with pain. Luis fondled the chips. He's spent enough time handling chips to make an accurate guess. A nod to John confirmed the loot to be ninety-five thousand give or take.

John stood with the fish in hand, "What do we do? It's not all here. We're still twenty five short." John pinned the man's elbows together behind his back.

"We'll just have to feed the fish to the shark." Luis stepped up and swung a knockout blow to the skinny gambler. John let the man fall onto the bed. Each brother grabbed a corner of the soiled bedspread and flung it over the unconscious man. Luis tossed him over his shoulder. Outside the bums and low lives meandered around, some looked but were not interested.

The view from Ducci's high rise office offered a unique view of both the intra coastal river to the west and the ocean to the east. A sun rose, pushing the night away. Ducci sat counting his chips. John and Luis stood before Ducci holding Gomez by the scruff. As Ducci neared the end of the playing chips Luis said, "We came up a little short so my brother and I decided to bring the fish to you." Ducci turned a stern look into a smile and threw a stack of twenties to the brothers.

"All in a days work gentlemen. Good job collectin' this fish." Ducci waved a hand and an associate came from the corner of the room. He escorted Gomez away.

John looked the cash over and handed it to Luis. "Wasn't much work at all, I guess it just comes natural."

"Is that so? Well you brothers are in luck. Anderson, one of my best collectors, was just killed the other day. That's why I was out on the street after this cheating rat myself. So I'm in need of another collector." Ducci leaned back in his chair reassured of his decision to send the untested brothers out after such an important fish. His reputation had been on the line every day that debtor ran around East Town blowing cash on unskilled bets.

"Just let us know what you want collected and we'll collect it." John said with his own sense of assuredness.

Luis fanned the cash. "Cause we can never go back to hourly work again." The brothers could see the light at the end of their hourly wage jobs and wanted it badly. This was a taste of freedom from uniforms and nametags. They would make money based on how hard they worked not how many hours they put in.

CHAPTER ONE

THE youthfulness from years earlier was gone, lost behind scars and the stories of how they got them. For the last eight years John and Luis had been living a life of tracking and hunting down the hardest thing on earth to find, a man who owes money to a boss. Their success was measured by the life of leisure they now lived. Sharing a suite high up in the Fabulous Beach Palm is just part of it.

The brothers came to live in the Fabulous Beach Palm when Sam Dennis (God rest his soul) had his then twenty two year old wife, Morgan, skip out on him. John and Luis, having left Sam's employ on good terms to be full time collectors, received the call.

The scumbag photographer who convinced Morgan she should be a model was easy enough to track down. He had an ad on Craigslist. A couple of emails were exchanged and a fake text message with a picture from one of the Beach Palm showgirls was all the bait required to meet with the pornographer posing as a legitimate artist.

In an apartment with blankets over each window and one on the floor, the brothers found Mrs. Dennis and the photographer. Morgan sat on the blanket with her knees tucked under her, with only a sheer

23

green tee shirt to cover her. The photographer danced around with a cell phone snapping shots telling her she was best he had ever worked with. She giggled and drank wine from a box.

The Collectors left with Morgan and the photographer was left with a smashed hard drive, cell phone, and simcard, anything that could hold a picture was destroyed.

Morgan returned to Sam with no one but the two collectors and the badly beaten photographer the wiser. This earned the brothers lifelong residence in the hotel. And Luis became the subject of an uncomfortable and never ending crush from Morgan.

Years after Sam's death the brothers continued to live in the hotel, mostly at Morgan Dennis' request. Each year Morgan convinced the brothers why *now* was not a good time to live elsewhere and offered them a suite one floor up. With a landlady as hot as Morgan and twenty-four, seven gambling an elevator ride away there was no reason to leave.

Though they now lived in a suite on the twelfth floor, their lives were spent on the casino floor. John sat with his elbows pressing into the stuffed leather edge of the craps table. His hands held his face up, his fingers tapped against his forehead keeping him awake. The youthfulness was gone from his face. A scar above his eye, slight crow's feet around his eyes and a fuller five o'clock shadow now aged him in the last few years since his days hauling money around the casino floor of the Fabulous Beach Palm Casino

Hotel. John's dirty blond hair was a short-cropped mess. His boots were scuffed and needed polish. His jeans were frayed at the cuffs.

He sat on a stool beside a craps table, a bored look on his face. The palms of his hands suspended his head, keeping him awake. Luis' tailored suit jacket was off and his sleeves rolled up. Luis threw the dice.

"What time is it?" John asked swiveling his head in search of a clock. "There's not a single clock in this place."

"Almost nine." Luis said without allowing John to distract him from the craps table.

"Winner, seven." The dealer called out.

"Nine?" John lifted his head out of his hands. "It's been over four hours. Four hours I sat here by myself watching you gamble. The girls left at like three this morning.....Man Luis, you're a junkie."

"We're both junkies, relax bro. Besides we can get more girls from the same place we got those two." Luis continued tossing dice without looking to his brother.

"The same place? You mean they were just hookin'. Man..." John frowned.

"What, it's not like that girl would have been your first time with a hooker."

"No, no it's not that. I just...I thought she actually liked me." John blew into his cupped hand. A sour look on his face signaled bad breathe. He unwrapped a stick of gum and popped it in his mouth. A young faced hotel attendant named Chaddick, brought over a small silver tray with the house blue tooth it. Luis had a call.

Chaddick waited until Luis had finished his toss. "You have a call Mr. Solo."

Before picking up the Bluetooth, Luis pulled out his cell phone.   No missed calls.   John shrugged, suggesting he find out who it was. Luis slipped the Bluetooth in his ear.

"Hello, yeah…"

The voice on the other end went on about something. John could only make out mumbles. Luis pinched his eyes. He had enough. "We don't hire out for that syndicate." He popped the Bluetooth out and flipped it onto Chaddick's tray. Luis added a blue and white chip to the tray.   Chaddick departed with a smile.

Luis remained quiet. He turned his attention back to the table laying down a stack of multi-colored chips.

John could wait no longer, "Who was that?"

Luis threw the dice.   Dealer called out a losing number. Luis placed a big bet again and tossed the die again and again he lost. His expression did not change. Turning down work while self-employed is not something successful entrepreneurs often do. Some jobs are too dangerous for any amount of money. To hire on with King Juan Miguel Lito, head of the Mexican Mafia in East Town, would increase the chance for a sudden death.

King Lito had never called on the brothers before to collect. He had his own ways of doing business and an army of soldiers to conduct it. Operations were always kept in house with undocumented workers coming and going across the U.S. Mexico border at leisure. There were just too many things to consider working for Lito. If the Collectors failed, they would be buried at sea or the swamps. If they succeeded but the job was too important for the Kings back in Mexico to find out about, the Collectors would be buried at sea or the swamps. Luis was smart to hang up the phone but this was not over.

"Chaddick! Come cash me out." Luis' smarts got the best of him. That call would not be a onetime thing.

Chaddick hustled over to the table to retrieve Luis' chips. Luis reached into his coat pocket and grabbed a pack of smokes. He shook the pack but nothing came out. He tossed the pack to the floor right at a Security Guard's boots. The large Guard wore the same uniform the brothers had in the past. The guard looked down at the pack. His face wrinkled at the corners.

"Get a good look at the brand and go get me some smokes."

The Guard backed down. He kicked the pack away with inept defiance. John was quick with a cigarette to calm his brother.

"Dude relax. Let's get some chow, I'm starved."

Luis nodded. Chaddick had a tray full of cash and few large denomination chips for Luis. He filled his pockets and shook off the loss at the table and the phone call.

"So what the hell was the call about? I've never seen you jack a play like that."

Luis stopped to light the smoke. He inhaled deep. "King Lito. He wanted to take a meeting."

John crinkled his brow. "King Lito? We've never–" He let the words fall off.

"I know and we're not going to either. Not for that psycho. Ever since Boss Ducci's rise, he and Lito have been locked in a cold war." The brother collectors managed to stay clean in the years they have been collecting. Boss Ducci gave them their break but in the last couple of years they have earned a reputation that has offered up employment with a variety of employers. They have chosen to play it safe and not align themselves with any one boss or enterprise. This has presented its own problems in the past but John and Luis made it work. Lately they lent their retrieval skills to collecting art or rare automobiles, objects people desire more than cash money. Together John and Luis had developed an uncanny skill for tracking, salvaging and returning just about anything anyone had lost or was taken from them.

"Working for Lito would put us in the middle."

"And heat up that war."

"Still," John shrugged, "I wonder what he wanted."

The brothers made their way to the front doors of the Beach Palm. The sun shone bright penetrating their dark glasses shrinking two pair of pupils and blinding the brothers for a moment. A sparkling fountain refracted the sun's rays along with every high dollar ride parked at idle waiting for its high rolling owner.

Despite the brilliant solar array the temperature outside was in the cool mid sixties. It was dead winter in sunny Florida. The natives wore parkas and the tourists wore shorts. John and Luis made their way to the valet across the salmon colored brick drive.

A V8 roared as it came to a sudden stop cutting off John and Luis from the valet. In the all black paint and tinted windows the brothers watched themselves in the reflection. All four doors opened in unison as large Mexicans in long coats exited. Shiny slicked back hair and trimmed goatees matched the black truck they arrived in. The man from the passenger's seat lead with a nickel plated pistol in his hand.

A heavy Mexican accent said, "King Lito wants his meeting." He hiked a thumb back toward the SUV.

Luis shook his head *no*. The four men opened their long coats revealing their armaments, two shotguns, one compact automatic and a shiny fifty caliber pistol.

Inhaling deep, Luis dragged on his cigarette. He took what was left of the glowing tobacco and flicked it at the man from the passenger's seat, catching him in the eye. The man swung his arm wildly at Luis' head. Luis caught the man by the wrist, twisted it and using the man's forward momentum, pulled him to the ground. Luis now had his own pistol out tucked behind the man's ear. The hammer clicked as it was thumbed back.

The other men went for their guns. John was quicker. His forty-five came out ready in a flash. "You'll never get a chance to use them." He said swinging the barrel between three close in targets. "Now let's go see the man that ruined my brother's play."

Diplomacy was not something that came easily to the collectors. In this case it was their only choice. Killing those men in the front drive of the hotel in which they lived would be bad form. Not to mention killing King Lito's men would lead to a blood bath and blowing up the hotel in the process. The brothers had their backs against the wall on this one. They would play tough but do as they were told.

CHAPTER TWO

THE entire black remnant was gone from Boss Ducci's hair leaving his head white with a few silver streaks. His weight was up and so were his taste for track suits. He sat smoking a cheap cigarillo and reviewed a spreadsheet tracking his loans. Along an adjacent wall a man sat with a shotgun looking out the floor to ceiling windows to the beach below. The wall across from the Boss' desk held three TVs. One broadcast financial news and interest rates, the other was a football game and the third was a simulcast Jai Alai game. Ducci looked up from his work. The number five Jai Alai player, Bernard, was up by three and they were about to enter the second round. Ducci thumbed his stack of tickets. Finding the right ticket for that game he saw his order was: 3/5/7. Bernard was supposeed to place or show, not win.

The loan shark grumbled and reached for the phone. On the other end a phone was answered in the player's locker room. Moments later Ducci watched as the five player lost, then lost again. Bernard ended the game with a show finish. It was Bernard's lucky day.

The intercom buzzed. Ducci slapped it, "Yeah."

"Boss, Tony Wren is here."

"How many times do I have to tell you dopes, Tony don't have to wait around here. Send him in." Ducci pulled his hand off the intercom and uttered a string of obscenities that got his guard's attention.

The electronic lock hummed, and then Tony walked through. He was lean, short and tan. His hair was a white blonde and shaped round by a perm. He smiled at Ducci and chomped his gum like it was a mouth full of grass. His white linen sport coat was open and a dark blue shirt failed to button all the way up leaving plenty of room for his gold chain to shine. Tony thought he was ready for South Beach. This was not South Beach.

"Tony, Tony how the hell are you? Philly too cold this time of year for ya?" Ducci said with a genuine smile, though he did not bother to get out of chair or extend a hand to shake.

"Ah Logan, I've been good ya know. God I love this Florida weather." He went to the window and looked down at the only people on the beach this time of year, old people walking the beach and Canadian spring breakers.

"That's great. So how's your momma?" Ducci said without looking up from his desk.

"Getting old and losing her marbles. Getting real batty. I'm sure your momma's the same." He finally settled on a chair across Ducci. One leg hung over the arm.

"Tony, she passed last year." Ducci lost his smile.

"Shit Logan, I'm sorry man. I remember now. I had to get my moms there for the funeral. I've just been so busy you know, this and that." Tony sat up from his too casual position. "See that's why I wanted to come see you."

Ducci sifted some papers on his desk. "What can I do for my cousin?"

"Well I got this new technology and looking for an investor." Tony said going back to smacking his gum.

Ducci shook his head no before hearing what it is. His cousin has used loan shark money for too many failed get rich quick schemes in the past. His younger cousin had to learn at some point hard work was the only to make it in this world. The one thing Ducci could not teach Tony was smarts, he believed you are either born with it or you are not.

"Tony, Tony. How many times have I told you there is no get rich schemes out there?"

Tony smirked, "Isn't that what you sell everyday with your twenty percent loans?" Ducci was surrounded by people hoping to get rich in this gambling town.

"To suckers and junkies, Tony. I built a fortune through cutthroat lending and collection." Ducci balled two fists that crackled as he constricted his fingers.

"What I have here will change all that. It takes a gamble and turns it into a sure thing." Tony reached into his right front pocket. He leaned in towards Ducci. "This little miracle here dials in on any electronic gambling device and automatically rigs it. A sure bet every time." Tony smiled.

Ducci's face contorted as he struggled to suppress the anger welling up from his idiot cousin. Ducci rose to his feet.

"Are you that brain dead Tony? My own flesh and blood so stupid. Why would I, a prosperous Loan Shark want to give junkies a winning hand?"

Tony sat red faced in silence. He had not thought this through.

"What will the gambling junkies come to me, for a fifty dollar loan? So they can turn that into fifty thousand dollars at every casino on the beach! It would be bad for business Tony."

Tony dug deep to fight for his cause, "Yeah but Logan look at how much more money you could be making off the casinos."

"You don't get it. Me and the casinos have a symbiotic relationship. I loan money to junkies, they lose it in a casino and I make it back with interest. Look, go back to Philly, its safer for you there with the family. Maybe try selling it in Atlantic City or someplace close to home. East Town is the wild, wild south Tony. If a casino owner gets wind of this you're dead."

Tony rose to his feet. Words caught in his throat. This was a sure deal that would finally allow him so lead way in the family, an enterprise all his own. It was the techie nerd addicted to Adderall that Tony supplied him who had come up with the cheating device. It was Tony who got the kid hooked on heroin then traded drugs for the device.

"Logan you ain't got no vision. I can sell this." Tony made for the door.

Ducci went back to his spreadsheet. He said "Tony I love ya like a brother but give it up. You're better off without it."

Tony waved a dismissive hand at his cousin and left.

CHAPTER THREE

THE black SUV cruised along East Town streets. The sun hung in the southern sky slipping beams of yellow between towering cement canyons that ran along A1A. Neon signs for casinos and gaming halls showed bright despite nature's best attempts. Each sign was different, some offered gaming others offered loans, all claimed to be the best.

On the street there was another contrast. Most are well dressed in polo shirts and cargo shorts and having a good time. Tucked back in the corners and alleyways wondered the down on their luck homeless, mostly former gambling junkies. A group of bums had gathered to throw quarters or some other game as the SUV passed. They needed to feed their addictions the best they could.

Over the bridge spanning the inner coastal river sat the mainland. A quick right and then another couple of blocks north the SUV stopped in front of *Flores Hermosas*. The façade of the flower shop was brick with green wood trim. A neon open sign blinked in ivy covered window.

The SUV pulled along back of the shop. The four Mexicans remained silent as they got out of the truck. John and Luis fell in line behind the leader. They have chosen their own fate now. No other recourse but to play this thing out and make the most of it.

Three of the Mexican gunmen moved around to the back of the truck. The rear doors opened and they removed something heavy duct taped in a blue tarp. The one from the passenger's seat pointed to the double brown steel doors of the flower shop. The brothers complied.

Inside the shop it was dark and cool, perfect conditions for the plants and flowers. The sound of tinkling water came from multiple directions. As the brothers passed swinging double doors to the main store they caught an eye full of King Lito. Lito was as wide as he was high, late forties, and Mexican. He wore a white shirt with a black tie tucked under a green apron wrapped high around his waist. Standing beside Lito was a widow clad in mourner's black. Lito picked out a bouquet for her. The widow, pleased, smiled and took the flowers. Lito looked back and spotted the Collectors passing. His expression changed from a sympathetic shop keeper to an artist glaring at a canvas unfinished. He twisted the pinky ring on his left hand and motioned them into the back office.

The office was small and over crowded with flowers in bloom. The air was cool, moist and sweet. Two TVs hung on the wall to the left of where John and Luis were forced to sit. One TV was split into four squares, creating four security monitors. The other

TV was running a muted tella novella. The brothers were more interested in the lower left square.

On screen, two of the Mexican gunmen from the SUV, dragged a rolled tarp trailing dark liquid. The third man came into frame wheeling a barrel over to the other two. He righted the barrel and removed the lid. The two men began to unwrap the tarp. The body of a man matching the age of the widow the brothers saw on their way in rolled off the tarp. His chest was stained dark and he lay with his arms and legs at forty-five degrees.

The two gunmen lifted the corpse and bent him forcibly stretching tendons and popping joints. The struggle to stuff the corpse drew the attention of the third man, as all three began pushing on the corpse. Unable to get the dead man in the barrel, one gunman walked off. He came back with an axe. The three men argued in overly dramatic fashion like that of a silent movie as they passed the axe back and forth.

Finally one gunman stepped up and dropped the axe separating the leg in two. At that point the corpse shot up. He flailed his arms, swinging them wildly.

The brothers jumped back in their seats while the movie played on. One gunman opened fire on the once already corpse. This time there was no coming back. That was when King Lito entered the office allowing for an echo of gunfire to follow him.

Lito waddled between the brothers and the televisions. He frowned, "Shot dead right in front of her." His accent was a stereo type from a western.

He glanced up at the screen then turned back to the collectors, "Well shot in front of her anyway." Looking back at the television with disgust he said, "Limpia ese enchastre!" His face then twisted into a smile turning him from mafia killer to ice cream man.

"I thought some nice flowers for the funeral would cheer her up. Bendigasu alma. I guess her husband should have paid his debts on time." Lito stretched short arms out to a humidor on his desk. Flipping it open he offered each brother a cigar.

John reached first, "I heard you had a thing for bad smells."

Lito sat back in his chair. He snipped the end of the cigar and lit it using a long stem match. "This is a bad smell to you? A Cuban? No, no my friends. It's the stink of people I cannot stand, especially dead ones. Yet I keep finding myself around them." The smile faded. A cloud formed around Lito. The room was silent except for crackling tobacco.

So far the attempts at intimidation failed on Luis. "Lito you called us here for what exactly?"

"I am a fan of the Collectors." Lito made air quotes when he said collectors. "It is a shame you have never worked for me. Up until now I have had no use for you. But, it seems I am in need of collecting something. There is a metallic briefcase. In it is $50,000.00 that is mine. A man by the name of

Tony Wren has borrowed my money and no paid me back." He grew silent for a moment then with fury he said, "I want him and his case full of my money collected and brought here to me." Lito slide a picture of Wren across the desk. John picked it up, looked and handed it off to Luis.

"So, why us? You have plenty of men working for you."

"You are the collectors, si?" He did it again with the quotes causing only to annoy the brothers.

Now it was John and Luis who sat quietly, no doubt thinking of how to get out from under the offer. Whether the display on the security camera was for the brothers' benefit or not, it confirmed all the rumors of the Mexican Mafia in East Town. Words like bloody and ruthless were just words. To watch a man get his leg hacked off and shoved into a barrel was something very different.

"Why the hesitation? You two want to be big time, no?

Luis put the picture in his pocket. John was concerned by his brother's action. What makes their partnership so great is how closely they think alike while on the job. Maybe they dress differently, chase after different women and drive very different cars but while collecting they fill in each other's gaps. There is no room for loopholes, gaffes or gaps in this relationship.

"Ten thousand dollars, five now and five when we get the money."

John lost sense of time and space as he recovered from the blow of his brother's offer. He looked up to the monitor at the hacked man in the barrel. Twenty percent on a collection was outrageous. The high bid was sure to be turned down, but just how forcefully worried John. His palms went wet.

Lito's eyes enlarged when he heard the bill for the collection. He must control his rage to finish the deal. His fingers drum rolled on the desk as the cigar glowed red. Lito calmed and leaned back in the chair.

Luis kept his eyes focused on Lito.

"Cono hijo de puta..." Lito muttered, then, found a calm volume for his voice saying, "Si, si. I will pay you what you ask. You have forty eight hours to collect, COLLECTORS." With a deal struck Lito left the office. One of the gunmen appeared from the corner of the room. He must have been there the whole time but went unnoticed with all the visuals going on the other side of the room. He rolled out onto the table two blocks of cash wrapped in blue cellophane, the kind used for wrapping flowers.

CHAPTER FOUR

THE suite on the twelfth floor of the Fabulous Beach Palm Hotel was large with white furniture resting in a sunken living room. To the left was the kitchen with a well stocked bar and beyond a hall lead to a bedroom. On the right side of the main room is another bedroom. Out through the large tinted windows a balcony and beyond the ocean. John dropped the cellophane wrapped money on a glass coffee table. He sunk back into the couch. Luis hit up the bar and poured a couple of whiskeys over ice handing one to John who sucked it back immediately. Luis sat across from John in a chair. Both men stared blankly at the wrapped money.

"I don't even want to count it. I have never *not* wanted to see five thousand cash in all my life." John got up and poured another drink.

"I didn't think he would go for it. I mean who ever heard of getting twenty percent on a fifty grand collection. I don't like working for that sadistic fuck." Luis shook his head then finished his drink. He went to the refrigerator and opened. Looking out of frustration more than hunger he passed on the room service leftovers.

Leaning against the bar John said, "Well, we're in it now. I'll start on the usual calls, then I'm hitting the sack. We haven't slept in about thirty hours."

Luis nodded though he did not feel like sleeping. He sat replaying the event over and over in his mind as if somehow focusing on it would allow him to relive it and change the outcome. But even then there was no sure solution out of it. The morning had started off good for the part-time gambler and full-time collector. Last night had been long and the company easy on the eyes. His play was up on the table and climbing. Morning brought the phone call. Other possible excuses to duck working for Lito played out through Luis' mind. He did the best he could knowing any other way and Lito would have dispatched his crew and it would be him in that barrel today. Now he was just over the barrel, but alive.

****

John came out of his room with a tee shirt in hand. He stretched while looking out at the sun coming off the ocean below before pulling the shirt over his head. Luis sat on a high stool at the kitchen counter, a little cup of espresso nearby.

"Man I must have slept over twelve hours. How about you?"

"Pretty much the same. One of those calls you put out came back on Tony Wren."

A woman with tanned athletic legs exited Luis' room, tugging down on a tee shirt. Her hair was a matted mess and she held a skirt in one hand. She paused when she saw John's gaping mouth. She turned to Luis and said, "Thanks... I ah..." She curled her lip and tugged down at the lower half of her shirt.

When no acknowledgement came, she huffed and stormed out slamming the door. John frowned and poured a glass of juice. He drank it down and wiped his mouth. The conversation continued as if nothing had happened.

"A call so soon? Who from?" John asked joining Luis at the counter.

"Marty. Yeah I know he isn't too stable but it's all we have to go on. Nobody else has ever heard of this Tony Wren. Marty called drunk around one saying he knew Tony was in town. Then he called back about three drunker saying he wouldn't tell us anything. You know Marty."

"Let's see if we can sober him up enough to get some kind of a lead on this Tony Wren."

Walking through the parking garage, John made his way over to his primer black 1950 Ford Coupe. It was a mild custom with the door handles shaved and an airbag ride leaving the front a couple inches higher than the rear.

Luis shook his head, "Not today brother. Let's take the caddy." He pushed the button on the keyless entry and popped the locks.

"I guess it is best," John conceded, "to put the wear and tear on your car." John looked longingly at his beloved automobile. A good deal of time had been spent (along with money) to get his ride looking and sounding the way she did. Every time a job came around it was Luis demanding to take the Cadillac, *his* Cadillac. The reason was the same, a black '50 Ford coupe was too conspicuous. They needed a car that was common in this elderly controlled city and the pearl Caddy fit that.

The drive through East Town was like many they had taken before. Up over the bridge, down US 1 a mile or two then cut west for awhile. The neighborhood they were looking for was out by the airport. It was a regular working class development. Most of the homes were moderately kept; all a pair of working parents had time for on a Saturday. Every five houses or so was a project of some kind. Wrapped in a blue tarp was time spent on the weekend whether it was a classic car or an addition to the porch, the job was never completed.

The Caddy pulled into the driveway of a brown house with a dead front lawn. The brothers got out of the car and walked to the door. Luis knocked but no answer.

John stuck his face to the window beside the door. Inside the house was a mess. The counter tops were lined with empty beer bottles, tables littered with pizza boxes and bottles of booze. One thing that was out of place for Marty was the opened briefcase filled with a white powdery substance. From John's distance he was not certain of what he saw. He waved Luis in.

Luis scanned the same dirty house. He spotted the coke and immediately headed around back of the house. Through the sandy top soil and past the gate they came to Marty's back yard.

There floating on an empty keg with the sun beating down on his pale behind was Marty. He was passed out. John reached into the pool and grabbed a volley ball. He fast pitched to Marty's salmon colored ass. With a holler Mary spiked up then rolled off the keg. He popped up rubbing burning eyes and flinging long curly black hair from his face. Marty's skin wrapped tightly around thin stretched muscle fibers. He had been a Jai Alai player until taking one to the face turned his left eye permanently swollen with scar tissue.

John pulled a towel from the back of a plastic chair and handed to him. Marty got out of the pool slinging a towel around his waist. He dropped himself into a plastic lawn chair. From the small matching plastic table he pinched a cigarette from a pack and lit it. Exhaling smoke from both nostrils, Marty looked up at the collector brothers.

"So what's up guys?"

"Tony Wren."

"Right, and I called you about that." Marty said more reminding himself than the brothers. "Right, right." He sat forward and rubbed his scarred eye.

46

"During the party, now I remember. Sorry last night did a number on my brain."

Luis kicked over a chair, "We're not interested in your coked up parties. We just want to know about Tony Wren."

"Coke?" Once Marty remembered he continued, "Oh yeah, well....yeah that... So Tony Wren...." Marty ran his fingers through his dripping wet air. "He's hiding out up in the north peninsula. Some empty motel called...um...that place is a real piece. He must be scared nutso to be hiding out in that dump."

"The name." John said in a calmer voice than his brother. "Marty what's the name?"

"Oh, Sunshine Motel."

"What else do you know about this Tony Wren? Does he have any ties, any allegiances?"

"Can't say, I never heard of him."

"Wait." John dragged a lawn chair over and sat across from Marty. "You never heard of this guy, I thought you knew everyone in this Sewer. Come on Marty, who is he?"

"Guys I swear. I don't know him. This kinda information just comes to me. I don't know maybe I'm all ESP and shit. Look, I give you guys tips on the dogs and Jai Alai and you provide occasional muscle when dudes don't pay up. We throw each other bones now and then. Believe me, this guy just showed up, said he wanted to place a bet on a game. He paid in cash, not chips, if that helps."

The Collectors knew they would not get anywhere with this washed up Jai Alai player. Marty was good for information as long as he remembered it correctly. Too many times the information he was paid for was buried in useless information, forcing the brothers to dig it out of Marty. This was all they had to go on, so they would need their shovels.

Luis stopped short of the gate. "Marty, don't you want your usual amount?" and threw paper clipped twenties at Marty.

Marty bobbled the catch and nodded a thank you.

CHAPTER FIVE

JOHN was behind the wheel of the Cadillac, gliding it along A1A and past the Sunshine Motel. The motel was located on the north end of town along A1A at the corner of residential street filled with close to death retirees. It was laid out in the standard L shape with twelve rooms facing A1A and the ocean. Sand blew off the dunes and piled in the corners of the motel. The grey weathered wooden fence in the back was collapsing in spots. The grass was tall and dead. Luis looked the motel up and down, noticing all the same things. No cars, no people moving about, nothing at all in front of the Sunshine except a for lease sign in the manager's office window.

The 7-Eleven sat across the side street and served as a good observation post.

They left the Cadillac parked in the shade of crossed palm trees. Each one took a second look at the foreclosed motel. No movement or signs of life.

Inside Luis headed to the cooler and grabbed a few Red Bulls and a few protein bars. John poured a Slurpee. He sucked the frozen soda through a straw while standing in front of a magazine rack near the window scanning the covers while taking a second to look to the motel.

Luis was ready to go standing at the counter. "All set?" he asked.

"Yeah the Slurpee and some nachos." John said holding the frozen beverage over his head so the clerk could get a look at the size.

Luis shook his head, having never intended to quench his brother's thirst. With a go-ahead nod from Luis, the clerk began scanning the merchandise on the counter.

"Anything else?" the clerk asked.

Luis placed his hands on the counter and peered through the scratched plexiglass countertop at scratch-off lotto tickets below. "Yeah...I'll take five of the Queen of Hearts and three Monopoly."

John put his Slurpee and nachos on the counter. "Man, Luis we live in a casino and gamble all day. And you're here buying scratch off tickets."

Luis snarled playfully at his brother.

The clerk remained emotionless, "Thirteen fifty-eight." Luis swiped his card and punched in his pin.

John leaned over the counter spreading his arms wide as he gazed down at the array of scratch off tickets. Each ticket longed to be scratched and reveal a winning combination of fruit or hearts or spades. "I'll take a few of those and a couple of these here." His finger mashed against the plexiglass.

"What a junkie." Luis said with a slap to John's back.

John and Luis settled into the Cadillac looking for any sign Tony might be there. It was still early in a collection the brothers wanted no part of. Adding to the unwelcomed anxiety placed on them by their current employer, the source of the information on Tony was sketchy. There were too many doubts lingering on this collection.

The motel remained quiet. Gusts of wind sandblasted the car. "John, did you think there was anything weird about Marty's behavior?"

John sucked the last of the Slurpee through the spoon shaped straw. "Yeah, I didn't know he was into coke. He had enough there to be a dealer. Maybe last night was his coming out party."

Luis smirked, "Yeah like a quinceanera for drug dealers." He always thought of himself to be the funniest one in the room.

"He was all jittery, even more than usual too. Maybe it was all that nose candy."

"Nah, it's not the junk. I thought the weird part was that he didn't ask to be paid this time. Usually he's all about the money before he even opens his mouth. Maybe he is dealing now and doesn't need our money."

The play list looped for a second time. The sun had moved from its highest point and now began to dip into the west. All the lotto tickets were clean scraped and the drinks emptied. Every so often the car would do a lap around the block up to the next convenient store for more caffeine.

The Cadillac was back in the original spot pointing towards the Sunshine Motel. John had opened the off track betting and simulcast apps on his cell phone. His finger flipped screens between the dog race in Dana and the horse race at Monmouth.

"Alright, the five came in. We're up like twenty five hundred."

Luis smirked but did not take his eyes off the motel.

John looked up from the simulcast race and over to Luis. "I'm thinking for the seventh race we do a trifecta wheel four, five, over the two, four, five, seven."

"Why don't you just box the eight dog supra?"

"I have bad luck with superfectas."

Luis shrugged. All the *up* and *down* dollar figures in gambling were not real to Luis. They were numbers in the imagination to build dreams on. The only real cash he was concerned with was the ten grand they foolishly accepted from King Lito. This was not money to have played with. The weight of finding the ghost known as Tony Wren weighed down on him more than his brother at the moment. Every man deals with stress in a different way.

Luis twisted the key and brought the Cadillac awake. "Tony could have made us. Let's go get some lunch and come back."

"Agreed, besides if Tony is in there, he's gonna wait till dark to go anywhere or come back from somewhere."

As the pearl colored Cadillac exited from the convenient store parking lot a black El Camino rolled in. The man behind the wheel pinched the lids of his beady Mexican eyes tight over his hooked Irish nose to better see the brothers leave. He mumbled something about luck and then a few swear words because those words made him feel tough. Rico watched the Brothers leave and then turned towards the motel.

John and Luis sat in a red vinyl wrapped booth that was mostly clean. Menus were stuck between the ketchup bottle and the napkin holder but the collectors needn't bother. They knew their orders.

Debrah, the waitress, in her mid forties with wrinkles around her mouth from thirty years of smoking strolled over with two waters. Judging by the condensation running down they had once been ice waters. The lunch rush was over by an hour and the Q-tip old timers had not ventured in for the early bird yet.

"What can I gitcha to start?"

"How are the burgers here Debrah?"

"Great." Debrah looked back at her only other table. Whatever was there, she found it more interesting than the pair in front of her.

John looked to his brother, "Okay, I'll have a *great* burger with cheese and whatever else comes on that. Oh and a coke."

"And you?" Debrah's attention went back to the table before her.

"Ice tea. Burger well done, just cheese and mayo."

"Either one of you want the salad bar?" The Brothers looked over to a dirty and rotten salad bar that stretched a whole three feet in length.

"No thanks, I'm on a diet." Luis rubbed his stomach.

Debrah pushed her pen into the pad but wrote nothing down. She sauntered away to put the order in. John unwrapped a straw and began to chew one end. Stakeouts always brought long draws of silence. Sitting in a parked car or in a booth at a diner exhausts even the most talkative person. John chose to watch cars pass the diner. Luis ran a finger across his phone checking the news - there was none.

The long silences allowed them time for pondering everything and anything. Many of life's questions were raised but seldom answered. This was one of those occasions to ask again.

John looked from the window to his brother. "So what do you make of this job?"

Luis pocketed his cell phone. "You mean the fact that Lito is willing to pay twenty percent and it has been way to easy to find the whereabouts of Tony Wren... I don't know, maybe it's always this easy working for Lito."

"True, but why would a guy who owes the Mexican Mafia money stay in town? That's what isn't sitting right with me." John fanned a hand across his face bringing up a smile, "Aahh... maybe we've just become too cautious these days. We should wrap this job up and take a vacation some place, you know, leave East Town or even the country. Sometimes I think we're as much junkies as the ones we're hired to catch."

"Leave town, and what quit gambling?" Luis matched his brother's smile.

"No, I mean, we really get off on collecting and the lifestyle it creates, cuz it's great, but I just think it's time to move on." John looked down at his now still hands. The paper straw wrapper was torn and twisted into pieces. Cupping his palm he made a small pile and pushed them to the edge of the table.

"We tried that and failed. Gambling, East Town, it's who we are." Luis stared at his brother who refused to look at him.

"Maybe we just focus on the collecting. We can collect other things, not just money and scumbags. What did gambling ever get us? Look at this town, look at us." John slapped the table rattling the silverware.

"It's because of gambling that we met and it's because of gambling that we live the life style we do. Don't forget that, brother." Luis did not want to give it all up like that. King Lito was just a bump in the road for them. Soon he would be gone and they could throw dice like they have always done.

Debrah arrived with the drinks and set them on the table getting the order wrong. John and Luis switched the drinks.

"You two friends of Tony?" Debrah's attention to her table finally came around. John and Luis looked surprised by the question. "I overheard you two talkn'."

"Yeah," John began the ruse, "of course we know Tony. You too?"

Debrah relaxed her shoulders and rested a hand on one hip, "I haven't seen Tony for a few days. You know he had that big investment deal today."

Luis not wanting to be left out added, "Yeah we heard. Pretty big stuff huh."

"Yep," the waitress' head bobbed with full knowledge of the inside deal. She was truly confident with what she knew. "He's supposed to come get me and take me out west with him. I've got family in Phoenix too. My shift ain't over for another few hours though." She looked up at a round clock with neon hands.

"We had some investments for Tony too, but we can't seem to find him. Is he still at the Sunshine?"

"Oh yeah...I didn't even think that place was still open till we, uh, he told me he was livin' there. Said his cousin owned it and that's why he could stay there during renovations or some shit."

"So which room did you say we could find him?"

"Six." The waitress said with no hesitation. Somewhere a bell dinged and without thought, she left the table in the direction of the bell.

Moments later she returned with two hamburgers. While the brothers switched plates and began to enjoy their made to order burgers... A few blocks away the muzzle flash from the window of room six drew no attention. No one on the block had their hearing aids turned up enough.

A man with slicked back oily hair and beady eyes laid the sawed off double barrel on the table. He grabbed a white washcloth from the bathroom and quickly turned it red, smearing DNA from his brown pleather coat. He emerged from room six and tossed the blood soaked washcloth behind him before closing the door. He made his way across the street to where he left the El Camino.

The only thing Rico could not wipe off was his smile. Teeth spread across his face, showing more as he neared his car. Once inside the El Camino his face changed. He looked down at the metal brief case on the passenger side floor. He slapped the steering wheel in disgust. The job had two steps. Kill Tony Wren and switch the briefcases. Rico called himself a professional, but he was not feeling like one at that moment.

Exiting the motel was clean. To go back with a shiny metal briefcase would draw attention Rico managed to miss. Facing King Lito as a failure was not an option, Rico grabbed the case and got out of the car only to immediately spin around and get back in. The brothers arrived in the pearl Cadillac.

The hatred Rico had for John and Luis Solo went back over eight years. Before the collectors arrived on the scene, Rico claimed the title of top collector in East Town. Rico held value over John and Luis because he was willing to take the jobs the brothers would not, kids, old people and killing. His favorite jobs were the ones that got messy, like the one he was on for King Lito, where a man needed dealt with in one way only. The brothers were not hired killers, though many times money was offered to do it. Rico was quick to lap up those jobs, but in doing so he was given worse and worse assignments as his reputation became tarnished the jobs lessoned.

Rico sat in his car bouncing ideas of what to do next when his cell phone rang. It was a blocked number from a burner phone but that was nothing new, all his incoming calls were. There were no saved numbers in phones in this business.

"Yeah." Rico said and listened to further orders. "I switched briefcases. The Solos are there now. Okay, I'll make the call."

The Cadillac slowed but never stopped when John jumped out. He made his way to one of the last pay phones in East Town. All the right motions were made to convince anyone who may have been watching that John did nothing but make a call. All the while his hands moved his eyes scanned the motel. The place appeared deserted, no car, no drawn curtains.

Rico sat low in the seat of his car. He could not risk John or Luis seeing him there. With the brothers now spilt apart, he did not know which one to follow so sitting was best.

The setting sun cast a hue of pink across the sky. Foot traffic along A1A began died off. Not a single car passed in several minutes. John hung up the phone and walked south. Moments later the Cadillac came back up A1A and swung into the parking lot of a vacant restaurant. Luis got out of the car and met up with John. Rico watched them each feel for what he knew was a gun. Without pulling them, the pair walked to the motel.

Luis headed for the manager's office while John went around the back. A six foot wooden fence backed up to the motel leaving little room for John to slide between. He had to turn his body sideways and shimmy along the fence dodging splintered steaks and rusted nails. If Tony or anyone else were to spot him there, the only option was to push through the fence and hope it broke apart. From the back of the motel John counted the frosted glass panes until he got to six. The correct room was easy to find, the bathroom light shown pale yellow through the frosted glass.

After jimmying the lock on the manager's office door, Luis found success as well. Sifting through dusty papers, Luis found contractor's blue prints for the motel. He looked over the floor plan of the motel. A single door adjoined room six with room five. A second entry point favored the brothers greatly.

John joined his brother in the manager's office. Together they laid out their plan. The sun was now nearly gone and so was the time they had remaining on this collection. King Lito would be calling soon looking for an update.

"The light is on in the bathroom of room six." John said with enthusiasm, something that had been lacking during this collection.

"Good, we've got the right place. Take a look at this floor plan." Luis spun the large blueprint 180 degrees. John leaned over the counter. It did not take long for him to come up smiling. He knew what Luis was planning.

"I'll take room five." John said.

"Sounds good." Together the brothers drew their weapons, with each chambering a round in their automatics. Once re-holstered, they exited. John went back the way he came, Luis stood up against the wall just out of view of the window of room five.

John found the bathroom window of room five broken. He climbed through easily. Inside the room it was dark. Remaining pink dusk seeped through the drawn drapes. John pulled them back. Luis peered in from against the wall. John threw up a hand to hold Luis in his place. He went to the adjoining door and listened. All quiet. He came back to the window and counted on one hand down from three. When his last finger curled completing his fist the collectors went into action.

John crashed through the adjoining door with his pistol out. At the same time Luis kicked in the front door. John went low while Luis went high. The room was empty and still. The only movement was that of dust particles through the rays of light crisscrossing from the bathroom. A dripping splatter drew the collectors' attention to the front corner of the room.

A man sat slumped in one of the two-chair dinette set. His arms hung at the sides of his still corpse.

Luis flipped on the light. The seated man had no face.

John came from checking the bathroom. He gagged on rising stomach contents when he saw the bloody oatmeal mess before him. Luis checked for a pulse despite the certainty. Once close to the corpse, he pulled a revolver tucked in the man's waistband. The gun he laid on the table. Next he removed a photo of Tony Wren from his breast pocket and tossed it on the table next to the pistol. The picture was of a man about forty five with curly hair nearly in a perm. A necklace on the corpse matched that of the one in the picture.

"I think this is Tony. By the looks of this blood splatter still dripping it's a fresh kill. Look, his pistol was still in his waist band. I'm betting he knew the assassin."

John leaned in and pulled a metal briefcase from the side of Tony Wren. "We got the case. Let's get out of here before the shooter or anybody else shows up."

"Don't you think we should call in this shooting?"

"And what turn it all over to the cops?" John said holding up the metal case. "You know what will happen, we lose our cut and King Lito will have a reason to kill us."

"Good argument, you should have been on the debate team in High School."

They left through the bathroom window.

Rico watched the Cadillac pull away from the vacant restaurant. He stood nervously waiting, hoping the next few minutes would play out in his favor. As he waited, another car pulled into the convenience store parking lot. It was a black Lincoln. Boss Ducci barreled out from the rear passenger door. Ducci's face was wrinkled with annoyance of the petty hired collector slash gopher that called him down. "Make it quick Rico." Ducci grumbled. Visiting this part of town was not something Ducci was in the habit of doing; there was not enough neon for him. Rolind, Ducci's driver, exited the car wearing a black suit and black driving gloves. A straight nose jetted out from his lower brow, pushing his eyes deep into their sockets. His stare was robotic, his actions finely tuned even to the expression he wore on his face.

Rico looked to Rolind then to Boss Ducci, "As I told you Boss, the brothers came for Tony. He phoned me and said that the Solos were after him. I just watched them leave." Rico pointed south, the direction the Cadillac headed. Among Rico's many self-proclaimed titles, liar was one of them.

"Damn it!" Ducci looked south towards the disappearing Cadillac. He looked back to the motel. "Let's go check on my cousin."

The men crossed the street.

Boss Ducci stood over the lifeless corpse of his cousin Tony Wren. It had been less than forty-eight hours since he last saw his favorite cousin alive, sitting in his office with another get rich scheme. Ducci thought back to the idea and wished he could have accepted his cousin's offer to invest in the gambling scheme - maybe it would have prevented this. There was next of kin to think of now, Tony had two daughters back in Philadelphia that could have benefited from their father's idea. He looked for the case.

The room was swept. A slow murmur built strength as it exited Ducci's lips. "Solos." Ducci swung a powerful hand smashing the lamp on the nightstand. The room went dark. Light from the bathroom cast long shadows on the men's faces.

"I want those Solo brothers dead! Rolind get the men together and get me all the cash I have. Collect on every fish, I want every cent of mine that's floating around out there brought in. Those Brothers are gonna have a price on their heads so high my own grandmother will crawl outta her grave to kill them." Ducci raised a clinched fist spotted with bits of embedded ceramic from the lamp. Blood dripped red down his wrist.

CHAPTER SIX

JOHN set the case on the coffee table with the same disdain he had for the cellophane wrapped cash. Next, he took off his jacket, sat on the edge, and chewed his lower lip. "It was stupid of us to take this case."

Luis poured some drinks in the background. Once the drinks were poured, Luis came and stood across the table. He took a swig, when the glass left his lips he said, "We need to get this case to Lito fast. Let's hope the whole fifty thousand is in there because one glitch could get our faces shot off too."

"There is no fifty thousand dollars Luis. It's always had to do with this case. King Lito stressed we get the case. He probably made up that story about Wren so we wouldn't get suspicious. We need answers that will only come from opening this case." John wiped sweaty palms along his pant legs.

"Okay. Sure open it, but tell me what could be in there that is worth dying over?"

"I don't know. Maybe naked pictures of Lito's fat wife or a note from his gay lover expressing his man love.....Hell if I know, either way we need to know if there is fifty G's in there or something else." John picked up the case and examined it with careful hands

64

like he was holding a baby. He ran a finger along the seam to study the lock.

"Lito's a psychopath John. If he thinks we tampered with it, we're dead men."

"If we're not dead already. We can't hand this case over until we know what's in it."

Luis gave in with a shrug, "Alright brother, it's both our funerals."

John fiddled with the locks. The metal case opened with ease. No bombs, no poison gas, John looked in and sat back on the couch with hands behind his head. He let out held breath. "I don't think that's fifty grand."

Luis looked into the case. Without conjecture, he walked over to the large sliding glass door and jerked it open. He stood smoking a cigarette allowing John to hypothesize. The bright neon lights of East Town reflected back off the silent ocean. He looked south to the boardwalk and pier. People, the size of ants, moved about. When the Solos were kids, the boardwalk was an escape from whatever tragic foster home they were placed in that month. Escape was on his mind.

"What the hell is this thing?" Inside, the case was filled with a block of grey foam. Little square cutouts nestled technical gadgetry. The largest piece resembled a standard stick flash drive. Next to it, in their own cut outs, were various sizes of adaptors with curled wires attached. John pulled the main piece and plugged in one adaptor at a time. With the third one plugged in the dimensions became apparent. He dug his phone from his pocket.

Luis snubbed the butt on the door jam and flicked it over the railing. "What are you doing now?"

John's face began to light up. He flicked his finger across the screen of his phone. He watched as the download indicator cycled down to completion. With a ding it was done.

"Well?" Luis now stood from behind the couch, over John's right shoulder. John continued touching the screen on his phone

"If this is...if it does what I think it does..." John said fully engrossed.

"What the hell are you saying?"

John bounced off the couch and made for the door. Luis was close on his heels shouting for more information.

The elevator doors could not open fast enough for John. He split sideways leaping through and stumbled out onto the casino floor. John paused in front of an IGT built slot machine. He chose the Double Diamond for his first experiment. He began punching something into the phone.

Luis caught up to his brother and grabbed his shoulder. "Slow down brother. What is going on?"

"Give me a chip." John held out a hand. Luis obliged. John slipped it into a slot machine giggling like a new born learning to laugh. The phone synced with the machine. As the fruit spun on the face of the machine a tiny version of it spun on John's phone.

66

Luis watched as the cherries went by three times before suddenly slowing and coming in line with the other two sets of cherries.

DING! DING! DING!

The slot machine went off with a clatter. Chips spilled out catching into the bucket and continued flowing until it was too much for the bucket and spilled onto the floor. John's giggle continued.

Luis remained statuesque. His face held no emotion, as if he were asleep with eyes open. Then a roar started deep in his belly. His lips parted and between white teeth came the laughter. He slapped John on the back and exclaimed "Amazing."

Luis said amazing a few more times before John grabbed a handful of chips and moved to roulette wheel leaving gray haired vultures to swoop in and gobble up the coins.

John dropped a stack of five chips on the roulette table. He then punched on the phone and in thirty seconds they win! The dealer pushed over a stack of green chips to the brothers. Luis picked one off the top and flipped it to the dealer. The rest he left to a floor attendant to send over to the cage.

Together the brothers stumbled into the casino bar laughing until their legs gave out. Plopping down on bar stools they cheered their success in discovering a way to beat the house.

"Dude we have hit it big!" John said slapping the bar.

Luis was breathing heavy trying to calm down from the laughter. "I know." He said, "We can hit every casino on the beachside."

"We'll be rich!"

As sudden as the laughter erupted for Luis is disappeared. His face went slack then said, "Yeah but this isn't gambling."

Enthusiasm faded from John's face. "Dude we can beat any house on the beachside and beyond with this little device. Just think Las Vegas, Monte Carlo. We can go places people don't know us and score every time."

Luis shook his head at his brother's lack of wisdom, "This," he said pointing to the small device, "is stealing. It's no different than if we just walked into the counting room and walked out with a cart of money. These casino owners are our clients and friends."

John took a deep breath and unplugged the device. He shoved it in his pocket and called over the bar tender. His drink order was for a shot of whiskey. Luis nodded for a round himself. They took their shots.

Between them sat the two shot glasses and silence. Then John said, "You're right. Just because the house always wins we know the odds and that gives us a small chance going into it." He stood up, "Well, it was fun while it lasted."

The Fabulous Beach Palm Casino parking garage had a designated floor to extended stay guests. John and Luis had long passed extended stay. It was with special permission of the now dead owner Sam Dennis and the new owner, the widow Morgan Dennis, that the brothers could live at a reasonable cost in the Beach Palm. They of course were obligated to perform special tasks for the Dennis'. The second collection of the then twenty one year old Morgan Dennis came when she had foolishly (as she later would describe it) decided to leave her seventy-year-old husband for eight months.

Sam Dennis was a wreck in the proceeding weeks, and allowed it to interfere with the casino. John and Luis had recently quit their jobs at the casino and were collecting full time. The work was steady and more importantly successful. The brothers decided to visit their old casino and gamble where they had never been able to gamble before. It was then that they saw the devastated hotel and casino owner.

Between the gambling brothers, John spotted Sam Dennis first. Sam's white hair wisped carelessly in the air and dreadfully in need of a shave. He was wearing a faded red t-shirt, navy dress pants and white Velcro orthopedic shoes. John mistook Sam for a homeless man who had made it past security to the casino floor. When Sam waved to the brothers, they recognized their old employer.

Sam forced a cheerfulness the brothers saw right through. He was quick to break the news of Morgan's departure. When the brothers asked if there was anything they could do to help, Sam took it as an offer to collect his young bride. Wanting to help an old friend who had given them a break once before, the collecting brothers agreed.

A few days hitting up some of Morgan's friends and acquaintances, the brothers took a drive to Tampa. They found the house of Jordan, the pot dealing new boyfriend. They had been warned Jordan was not a guy to mess with because he had been to prison. The brothers laughed it off, all that meant to them was that Jordan was stupid. None the less, when it came time to hit the house they did it fast and hard.

Jordan and Morgan sat on the couch in the middle of the day watching bad reality TV when Luis kicked open the front door. Jordan ran for the garage but John was standing in the doorway. When Jordan ran for the stairs, Luis body checked him into sixty-four inch flat screen. Charcoal colored glass splintered and covered the tile floor. The ex-con drug dealer lay on his stomach refusing to look the home invaders in the face. He told them to take what they wanted and that all the pot was upstairs in the guest room.

Morgan sat silently on the couch. She wore a thin yellow t-shirt with two darkened ovals letting all three men know what she was not wearing underneath. A gentle smile soon crossed her face as she recognized Luis. It had been a year since she last saw him but he had that kind of effect on women. She stood up and lifted her arms out for a hug saying "Luis, good to see you." She got one arm around his broad shoulder when he blocked the other.

"It's time to go Morgan."

Jordan lay on the floor confused. His brow creased as his brain worked overtime processing the invasion. He had assumed they came for him and his drugs. Morgan left with a blown kiss to Jordan who never saw it, John made sure of that. He did not have to but wanted to.

When Morgan saw the condition Sam had deteriorated into at her absence, she recommitted her vows on the spot.

The brothers were rewarded with a place and a suite one floor up.

The Cadillac was in its usual spot. The brothers made their way to the car and got in. John put the case between his knees on the floor. Luis was slow to press the ignition button. John did not have to question his brother on the slow start, he was feeling it too. Neither of them wanted to face King Lito and turn over the case. On the surface everything was calm; they completed the assigned job with time on the clock. The apprehension for John was the memory of Tony Wren sitting still with no face, for Luis it was the ease at which they found Tony. A man running from the Mexican mob is not an easy man to find. For Tony to have stayed in town meant there was something more to the collection than fifty thousand dollars. The question had to be asked again, what had they stumbled upon and just how valuable is the little bit of technology in the metal case. Neither of them spoke out loud.

From the rear of the driver's side, a man in a shiny metallic blue suit approached the car. Luis caught a glimpse of the man before he was to the window. He stood, not bending and asked, "Are you Luis Solo?"

"Yeah, who wants to" Luis did not finish his sentence before he got a nickel-plated revolver shoved in his face. Luis grabbed the gunman's wrist and thrust forward further into the car. The man's face rammed into the Cadillac's upper door jam. Luis then pushed up on the man's gun arm breaking it at the elbow. John pulled a boot knife and jammed it through the gunman's hand into the dash of the car. The pistol bucked and everyone's ears rang as a bullet punctured the lower corner of the windshield. The pistol dropped. John punched the ignition of the Caddy. Luis dropped it into gear. The tires screeched and burnt as the car leapt backward.

The gunman was dragged a few yards before falling from the car.

John held the pistol while looking out the rear window of the Cadillac for any pursuers. "It doesn't look like we're being followed. Who the hell was that?"

"I'm guessing a hitter."

"Say it ain't so."

Luis turned to his brother, "It wasn't one of Lito's. That guy wasn't Mexican, he only uses Mexicans. Brings them over the boarder for a job and then sends them back. My money is on whoever killed Wren and knows we have the case."

"This job just got a whole lot worse." John opened the glove box and pulled out a few napkins. He wiped down the pistol and dropped it out of the speeding Cadillac. He looked down at his crimson stained hands. Blood had seeped into all the cracks and crevasses. He spat on both his hands and wiped them with more napkins. "Limitless roulette in Monte Carlo sounds so good right now."

They agreed without speaking that going to King Lito's flower shop was off the table. Luis steered the caddy south along A1A until they got to the Thunderbird Hotel and Casino. Every room large enough to fit two people in East Town was labeled hotel and casino. Across the thousand-bulb marquee was the name Trip McGavin, performing live, shows at 4:30 and 7:30.

Ticket sales for the Thunderbird Theater placed thirty-five people in the audience, less than half that were present when John and Luis entered stage left. Trip McGavin closed with his cover of *My Way*, a song he brought all the way to number ninety eight on the on a recent blogger's poll of the top covers of the 1960's.

Trip McGavin had been a top forty singer in the years before the City Council of East Town turned to gambling as a way to reinvent their town. In those days, he would get on stage and sing all night. He had the look, straight white teeth made brighter by a dark tan, perfectly permed hair on his head and sprouting from his chest. His charming smile and voice that melted hearts and ruined marriages got him magazine covers and guest spots on hit television shows. At the close of the show, a three foot mound of woman's undergarments and room keys would be swept off stage.

Back then, as now, Trip McGavin was friends with everyone. He signed autographs and flew across country to sing for sick kids. He also befriended club owners of the clubs he sang at, often times staying after hours for private sessions and even visiting their homes for birthday celebrations. Many of these club owners did not so much own the club as they did control it. Money was paid to these men for operating costs and a certain amount of protection.

Trip McGavin walked a fine line with his friends, similarly in the way the Solo brothers were managing. Trip managed to stay friends with everyone and afforded him inside information, the kind of information the Solos needed.

After taking a bow to a half engaged audience, he motioned to the Solo brothers to meet him back stage.

A security guard dressed in dark blue cargo pants and long sleeve shirt stood between the Solos and Trip McGavin's dressing room door. His nametag read Gill and his unevenly trimmed goatee wiggled when he said, "Hey now fellas. I can't let you in there." His hand went up.

"It's okay, we're friends of Trip." John said believing it was enough to brush past the guard and enter into the dressing room, but Gill's other hand went up.

"Sure ya are. Now I've told you once. You fellas can't be back here."

"He will see us. Just tell him -" Luis started with a smile but Gill was not flattered.

"Listen up." Gill barked while grabbing at the radio strapped to his shoulder. "I have orders from the man himself. I'm authorized to use force."

John grabbed the guard's wrist nearest the radio and shoved him against the wall with a forearm across the man's neck.

Luis leaned in close to the Gill's ear, "Now you listen. You just tell Trip the Solo brothers are here and need to speak with him."

The security guard's eyes rolled down to the hand holding him. The hand looked like it had been dipped in rust colored paint and left to dry in the sun. With limited movement of his head and neck, Gill managed to nod saying, "Brothers huh. Okay I'll let him know."

John released the guard, allowing him to turn and knock softly. Moments later, the door cracked. Gill whispered to the person inside. The door closed then opened revealing a tall with blond tightly wound hair and glasses that horned in the corners. She wore a powder blue dress and a black headset.

She held a pleasant thin lipped smile and said, "Mr. McGavin will see you now." Holding onto the doorknob with one hand, she swept the other across her slender waist and held it out for the brothers to enter. She shut the door in Gill's face.

Trip McGavin was seated in a makeup chair with his back to the Solos. His face lit up in the mirror as the brothers entered. The dressing room was large with three makeup chairs and couch backed against the wall behind them. Trip finished blotting his face with tissue paper before standing to greet the brothers with a handshake.

With the pounds of stage makeup whipped away, Trip looked like any other sixty something year old man who enjoyed the self-tanner. The show kept him fit, working up a thirst.

"Natasha," Trip said to the blond in the blue dress, "How about getting us something refreshing?"

"Sure thing Trip." She turned to the brothers and waited for their order. "A couple of scotches coming right up. Trip, another Bloody Mary?"

Trip bobbed his head.

"No Scotch, give up drinking Trip?" Luis asked taking a seat alongside his brother on the couch.

"I had to start taking care of myself Luis, I'm not getting any younger, but I couldn't quit all together." Trip took a seat back in the makeup chair, and spun it 180 degrees to face the Solos. All three men watched Natasha leave the room for the drinks.

"Good girl you got there Trip." John said with a grin.

"Yeah but it's strictly professional."

"Sure just like the last three assistants you married."

"Nah, this time it is. I used to date her mom. Natasha's more of a daughter to me." Trip covered his grinning mouth with a hand. "Or more of a second cousin twice removed." They share in the light humor.

"It's good of you to see us." Luis said bringing the conversation back to point. "We're in something deep, but you probably already know that."

"Yeah, yeah." Trip pinched his eyebrows together, "I heard some things today. I figured...." Trip glanced down to John's blood encrusted hands. "John what happened to your hand?"

"Oh that.....Not my blood." John wiped his hand on his pant leg.

"Good, anyway I figured you guys would come around. It's best we speak in person. First you better get me caught up and then I will tell you what I know."

Before Luis or John could begin to tell Trip the events of the past forty hours Natasha returned with the drinks. The glasses were distributed with thanks given in return. Natasha went about her usual duties. She opened a laptop and began navigating a few social networking sites with inflated news from tonight's show.

The three men remained quiet while Natasha worked. Then Trip cleared his throat...then once more before Natasha looked up from the computer,

"I'm sorry did you men need to be alone?" she said looking through horn-rimmed glasses. "I'll update your blog from the other room." She stood with a smile for John and Luis, took the laptop and left the room through a door in the rear.

Trip shrugged, "She's leading my come back."

"Come back?" John questioned sarcastically. "I never knew you left."

"Getting back to why we came," Luis said again directing the conversation, "King Lito hired us to collect a briefcase with fifty grand in it. We didn't want the job so I told him twenty percent for collection and five up front."

"That's kinda high isn't it?"

"We thought he would turn us down." John said.

"Smart way to get out of it."

"If it had worked. We should have known that twenty percent for fifty K was going to be a dangerous job. What do you know about a guy named Tony Wren?"

"Tony." Trip mauled the name over in his head. As a celebrity, he traveled frequently and met hundreds if not thousands of people while on the road. Trip's star may have tarnished but that only made him more of an institution. In the bigger towns, when Trip McGavin went up in lights, people turned out for it. "I remember him, barley, kind of a dunce that one. I met him a few years back while playing a gig at one of Trump's places in Jersey. He's connected up in Philly. He comes out to Atlantic City and plays like he's a big shot because no one really knows him. Is Wren mixed up in this?"

"Connected." John mumbled. He had to say it aloud for proper processing. Connected meant all kinds of trouble. Even if Tony was not high up as Trip described him.

"Wren was the guy with the brief case." Luis refused to accept the weight of that information and the worry it brought.

"Was?"

"Was," Luis swallowed the last of the scotch. "He was a guy with a face too. Someone got to him just before we did and blew his face off. They either weren't after the case or ran out in such a hurry they missed it. We are hoping you could fill in some gaps."

"Sorry boys, not because I don't know anything, sorry cause I do. First off, that connection of his is being close cousins with Boss Ducci. Tony being mixed up in this would be news to me. I got another name for you, Rico Sullivan. If you know him, you know he's a free lancer, highest bidder type. If you go after him be careful he looks like a simpleton but he's a pro."

Luis and John looked at each other. Rico Sullivan was a name they recognized. His involvement did not make much sense to the pair of collectors. They had run into Rico while mixing with Ducci's crew. The brothers always made it a point to stay away from him. The last news on Rico was that he skipped town with the cash from a big collection for a Shark trying to make a name for himself by lending too much.

"Rico." Luis said with a mouth of vinegar. "We know the guy. I didn't think that weasel was back in town."

"Let's go find him." The brothers stand, as does Trip. "Thanks Trip for helping us out." Hands were extended once more.

"No sweat kid. You guys were there for me when I needed that little something collected and you got it back discreetly. You came through for me and I return the favor. Wish I could tell you where to find Rico."

"We'll find him. We always do."

"If he doesn't find you first. I'm afraid there's a battle royale brewing between the bosses. Judging by the blood on your hand John I'd say you two are right smack in the middle of it." Trip's gleaming white teeth were covered up by pressed lips. No one likes to be the bearer of bad news.

CHAPTER SEVEN

THE moon cut a swath of pale grey light through the middle of the black Atlantic. On the eleventh floor the moonlight came through the floor to ceiling sliding glass doors. Lining the walls of the office were men dressed in suits off the rack, shirts that were too big and pants too slim. The ages of the men ranged from just out of high school to just collecting social security, but not many between those ages. One man was, Mr. White. He sat in the corner of the room reflecting the sole light source in the room from off his pale baldhead. From behind the amber lenses in black metal frames, his eyes took on an eerie red hue. His suit was tailor fit, with a little extra room to conceal the large caliber handgun strapped to his hip.

Logan Ducci sat in his overstuffed leather chair. His fingers went from intertwined to tapping on the wood surface of his desk back to intertwined again as sweat beads broke across his brow. His busy hands found a handle on the top drawer. A metal case lay open. Five glass syringes lay suspended in grey foam. Each of the syringes was filled with blue colored liquid. Beside the case is a Ziploc back full of sugar cubes. The red contents were injected into a sugar cube. Ducci popped the cube in his mouth. With a deep soothing breath, he pushed off the mahogany desk bringing his large frame upright. Slowly he wound in-between the various thugs that stood motionless in his office.

"Maybe fifty grand wasn't enough for you guys. Maybe the murder of my flesh and blood wasn't enough either." Ducci's lip quivered, not from the suppression of grief but of the drug working its way through his blood stream. Ducci circled back to the desk and went for a cigar. Rolind was quick with a lighter burning the end of the tobacco. Ducci made a few quick puffs and approached a man in a tattered blue suit. His hand and face covered in rust soaked bandages.

Cigar smoke plumed adding a silver tint to the room. "Do I pay that well? I pay so good that none of you as much as flinch at fifty G's anymore!"

"Boss," the man in the tattered suit began in a bedside tone, "I had them but -"Ducci heard enough and drew a revolver from a belt under too much tension. He pointed it at the failed hit man. "There's .08 pounds of pressure on this trigger. Is that too much for you, any of you?" Ducci fanned the pistol along the faces of the henchmen he hired to hunt the Collectors. The barrel centered back on the man in the tattered suit. Ducci fired one round. The man did not have time to turn or utter a sound. He fell back into the arms of the henchmen behind him, as in a game of *faith* the men caught their comrade.

"Get him out of here!" Ducci turned back and let the pistol drop on the mahogany desk. He turned slowly, expecting to find the room nearly empty. Instead, his men remained, "Go out there and kill those collectors!" He spun grabbing the pistol and flung it around his large frame. The men climbed over each other to get out of the room. The last two men dragged their fallen comrade out with them.

Only Ducci, Rolind and White remained in the office. Rolind put a paper bag with the outline of a large brick onto the desk. White sat motionless in the corner. Slowly and deliberately, he raised his 6'6"frame. With one long stride he covered the distance to the desk. Without looking inside, White stuffed the bag into his front pant pocket.

"White this is for the job in Canada. I will triple that if you kill the Solos." Ducci sat back in his chair. His eyes do not make it all the way up to White's face. It is better this way for both of them they do not.

White's response was a low growl. He looked out the window at the beach below. In a few hours, the sun will be out and the white sands will be crawling with people lathered in suntan oil soaking up the rays. "I hate this town, it's too sunny here." The beach was no place for an albino suffering from alopecia.

Boss Ducci looked to the fresh brown stain on his berber carpet. "Okay seventy-five isn't enough, how about one hundred?"

White remained silent.

"Two hundred and fifty thousand dollars a piece. I'll pay you by the minute to torture those bastard brothers so you take your time and make them feel every one of their last miserable minutes. Got it Freak?"

White snarled once more. He shifted his weight. Calculations zipped through his mind. Contemplations of biting the hand that fed him. In that second, every possible scenario of him killing Ducci and Rolind and leaving with the money crossed his mind. He chose life. With a nod, he accepted.

CHAPTER EIGHT

THE Cadillac drifted aimlessly up and down, back and forth all across East Town streets. The brothers knew the town better than most, but tonight was about finding direction. Night had fallen and so have their hopes of a clean collection for King Lito.

"So where do we find Rico?" John picked at a hangnail. Two fingernails had already been nibbled.

"Don't know, never collected a collector before. Do we know anything about this guy?"

"Just that he is a dirt bag who takes the lowest bids for his work. You know the jobs we wouldn't take, kids and old people."

"I'm betting that was Rico back at the Sunshine Motel."

"Even money on that. We know he's a perv and we know he just got paid. I know someone who would know where to find Rico." John dug in his jeans for his phone. "Pull in here I need a Slurpee."

The Cadillac parked in front of a brightly lit convenience store. John had his cell out dialing. With the other hand he gave Luis two crumpled up bills. Luis grumbled then went into the store.

"Laticia. Hey it's John Solo. Yeah, uhuh. I know I'm sorry I haven't been by to see my Brown Sugar."

He laughed as Laticia responded with an endearing racial slur of her own. "Hey I need to find a guy and you might know him. He goes by the name of Rico Sullivan." There was a long pause on John's side of the conversation as Laticia let out a list of unflattering words to describe Rico.

He cut her off to keep her on track "Yeah okay. But where is he now?" Silence. "Yep, we'll try there. Call me if he comes back. Okay..... Alright." John smooched into the phone, "And put that where ever you want." John ended the call just as Luis reentered the car. Luis handed over a Slurpee but no change. John frowned. Luis cracked a can of liquid caffeine.

John chewed the end of his straw before sticking it in the Slurpee. Between slurps he said, "Laticia said she knows Rico. He's not allowed in most of the clubs, gets violent with the girls. He was in tonight with lots of cash burning a hole in his crotch. The managers looked the other way while he blew his wad."

"Was in, so that means Rico's gone."

"He's not at the Head Turner any more. She said Rico left but wasn't done for the night. We should try Pav-Luv's."

It did not take long to reach Pav-Luv's. A pink neon dog hovered above the one time book store. Beside him a brightly lit yellow bell blinked creating a side to side motion of the bell. With each blink of the bell a neon lit tongue grew from the dog's mouth. The windows were covered over with life size images of the women who have danced there though no living or dead customer ever remembered the blond in window three and the brunette in five ever dancing.

Parking was around back and so was the entrance. It cost each brother five dollars to pass through to the darkness of the bass thumping, smoke filled club. To the right, three neon wrapped stages lined up parallel. The middle stage stretched longer by a half dozen feet and stood a foot higher. Along the left wall was the bar running most of the length of the room. Beyond that was the hallway leading to the champagne rooms.

It was still early. The club held only a few patrons watching as homely and other wise unemployable strippers took off their clothes. The uglier the woman the more skin she showed. Luis walked to the far end of the club and grabbed a seat with a vantage point of the whole club. He lit a cigarette and ordered a drink from a girl with a feather in her hair and tassels over her nipples.

John headed to the bar. Behind the bar was a man with one cauliflower ear, scars along both eyebrows and slight scars on his knuckles. John looked back at his brother. They locked eyes for a moment, which was all they needed to transmit to each other this bartender could be trouble. John ordered a drink, plucking a bill from a wad of folded cash, letting the wad linger so the bartender and strippers on break could see. A girl clad in a Chinese Dragon print dress, not much more than a sheet of silk, saddled up on the stool beside him. Her black hair was twisted up in a bun with a chopstick holding it. Jade stopped talking to her Bo, brining her attention to John, batting eyes with excess eyeliner giving the illusion of slanted eyes.

"Hey dare goo rooking." Her accent was thick with pigeon.

John kept his eyes forward looking into the mirror behind the bar. He sipped his drink then said, "How are you doing?"

"Buy a ger a drink?"

"Oh I'll do a lot more than that." They laughed together as John threw a twenty on the bar. The bartender scraped the twenty away and poured a drink without asking her order or giving change.

"I'm guessing you come here often." John said as the forced laughter faded.

"You a funny man. I rike funny man." Jade continued her ruse.

"Here's a joke. Ricco Sullivan. Ooppss... damn that's the punch line. Know where I can find him?" John slowly counted out five twenties but kept a hand on them.

"Are you a cop?" the accent was gone weakening the clever eye makeup. She appeared less Asian. John shook his head no. Jade put her hand on top of his on top of the bills. "He's here, in one of the champagne rooms." She rose what little silk covered her upper thigh to reveal a purpling bruise.

88

John eased his grip on the money. It disappeared quickly somewhere in the skimpy silk dragon. John downed his drink and made his way to his brother.

"He's here."

Luis had his eyes glued to the stage. A stripper gyrated, twisted and rolled. Through all the motions, she kept eye contact with Luis who flipped a gaming chip on the stage, joining two others.

"Bro I said he is here. Now let's go get this son of a bitch." John stood alone within arm's reach of Luis and the girl on stage holding his brother's attention.

Luis held up a hand to pause John, "Dude you have to see this." Luis dropped a stack of chips on the stage. The stripper dropped down on the chips with her butt. The chips disappeared. Luis smiled and nodded at the stripper's trick.

John was not impressed. He came for the man that set them up, not washed out strippers and their Hep-C. "That's great but can she give exact change?" John slapped his brother on the back. Together they made their way back to the champagne rooms.

Three red doors each hung cutouts of champagne bottles turned right side up letting everyone know they were occupied. Beyond each of the doors a customer got as far as the stripper and his wallet would let him. If the collectors rushed the wrong room it would alert Rico and give him the upper hand to either escape or let the brothers have it in the face like Tony did.

A break came when the door of room three opened. A stripper with clip-in hair extensions falling from her stringing dyed hair stood in the doorway. She was looking back at Rico who was seated in the center of the room in a red velvet chair. The chair was spacious with broad arms. He shouted something about getting him two more girls and another drink. As she passed the brothers, the pair caught sight of rose blotched hand prints on her pale skin. She shot them a heartless smile as part of her phony uniform.

They let the door close without Rico catching sight of them. John nodded confirmation to Luis. Luis dug out a pair of leather gloves. John pushed open the door. Luis rushed Rico before the thug could get out of the velvet chair.

John shut the door quickly. Rico, startled, tried to stand but was slammed back in his seat with a hard punch coming down on him.

Rico grabbed at his aching jaw, "Ahhhh...what the fu." Another punch came from Luis. Rico faked a wince. For Rico, taking a beating was part of the job. It was a headache or lower back pain for most, for Rico it was a couple good punches in the face.

"Keep your mouth shut Rico." Luis pointed a gloved finger at Rico.

John leaned in on Rico's swelling eye. He gave Rico a quick pat down, discovering a pistol and tossing it to a corner of the room. Luis began to pace back and forth like a caged animal, tugging on his leather gloves keeping them taught.

"Hey, John....I don't know" Rico shifted in the chair.

Luis threw another punch down on Rico's already swollen eye. Like a tic with a belly full it popped sending blood splattering. This time Rico winced for real.

"I talk first, got it." John was back in Rico's face. "If you utter another sound out of turn Luis will make your face look like chewed bubble gum. Now, who killed Tony Wren?"

"Is that what this is about? I don't know him." Rico's left eye was shut. Blood had cascaded down the side of his face and soaked into his shirt. Rico's one good eye focused in on Luis who stepped in with a recoiled leather fist.

"Okay, okay. Let me think....Tony...." Rico clicked his heels together releasing a small three inch rusty blade from the tip of his right boot. The bass thumped through the walls.

"I know Tony. I met him leaving your whore of a mother's house."

John's face registered surprise. Rico had more balls than either brother took him for. It just angered Luis who dropped another angry punch. A tooth from Rico's mouth flew to the floor. Rico watched it land. He lifted his boot slicing open Luis' pant leg and cutting the thigh. John grabbed Rico in a choke hold from behind. Rico kicked violently with the bladed boot then went limp from lack of oxygen.

"How bad is it?" John gave one more tug on Rico's neck before being fully satisfied he was out. Luis was on the sofa looking at the hole in his pant leg. Blood seeped into the linen pants.

"It's not deep. He's got a little blade. No wonder he beats the girls."

John kept a distance as he examined the blade. Looking back to Luis he said, "You'll need a tetanus shot to be safe. God knows who's been stuck with that shiv."

The door to the champagne room began to open. John rushed the door putting a shoulder into it. From the other side of the door stood a scantily clad cow girl. Her hair was twisted into two braids covered by a straw hat. A lasso was draped over one shoulder and she had on a sparkled red denim vest and daisy dukes. John pulled out a few bills.

"Sorry sweetie, Rico doesn't like girls anymore."

The Cowgirl snatched the cash without question. She turned and started back to where it was she came when John called to her. "Hold up a second. He might still want to be tied." John took the rope from the Cowgirl's shoulder and closed the door. Walking back John technically and specifically flipped the rope around in his hands.

With one foot over top of Rico's blade wielding boot, Luis used Rico's own belt to bind his legs together. Luis got out of his hunch and slapped Rico until he regained consciousness.

Rico's good eye rolled in the socket, his other eye was completely swollen shut. His knees came apart as he tested the strength of his binding. It held. This was just one of those things he had to wait out. Situations like this kept Rico on the road from town to town. Rico found double crossing was the easiest way to turn a buck. Getting beat to a pulp was just time in service.

The beatings were not over. Luis stood over Rico. "Rico start talking."

Rico bobbed his head down and came up with a smile. "Might as well tell you two everything, you're dead men anyway."

"Is that so?" John had the rope looped in his hands.

"Yep, if the bounty Ducci put out doesn't kill you two for Tony's murder then Lito will because that's the kinda guy he is."

Rico could hear the stomachs of the collectors hit the stained floor. A warmth filled him stealing away the pain from his swollen eye. The news that Boss Ducci, the man that gave them their start, now put a bounty on their heads, put a lump in their throats. Rico might as well as jumped up and smacked them each with a baseball bat.

John's eyes went round as his eyebrows arched saying, "This guy is full of shit." John shook his head. He chose to deal with the news by denying it.

Rico laughed. "You guys really don't know."

Luis dropped a left bloodying Rico's lip. Blood seeped from both corners of Rico's mouth, like a vampire who had just feasted. A tongue snaked out to lap up the corners, smearing the blood. The knuckles of Luis' gloves were stained. He often dealt with frustration through violence. Being a foster kid with a bad temper equaled several homes. By age thirteen he had been in as many homes. It was not until the home where he met John that the rage was able to be checked. It was John's ability to laugh every time Luis got angry that changed his strike first policy.

John slapped his brother on the shoulder. Luis spun and walked off his rage. "Ducci wouldn't go for a gambling fix, he would be out shark money if that little tech trick wound up on the market."

The hand that had fed them for so long was now hunting them. A collection was out on their heads and turning up with the money would not clear the debt.

"So you set up the meet for Tony and Lito?"

Rico nodded, "Yeah I played middle man."

"And when negotiations went south, you played middle man once more pinning Tony's murder on us."

Rico's smirk revealed a gap created by a missing tooth. "Something like that. It's all your fault anyway. The famous brother collectors. You made yourselves the target." Rico was glad to be a part of the hit on the collectors. The real icing was being the guy to tell them they were dead men. His mood was light. He was confident knocking out a tooth was as far as these two collectors would go. The ability to get the job done with the least amount of damage to the collection ensured more business. The gambler would be more likely to borrow from a shark if the collection went smooth and no one got beat to a pulp.

When John swooped in with rope, Rico's eyes went big with one question. The Collectors never went this far.

John tossed the noose he had tied over a rafter. The loop slipped over Rico's head. A smile of disbelief remained on the killer's face. John jumped, gritting his teeth as he pulled down on the rope lifting Rico off the chair. Finger nails scraped skin and hemp as Rico dug his fingers into his neck to open an airway. Luis threw a final punch and Rico ended his struggle.

Whether Rico's body had been discovered or not did not weigh on the Collectors minds. Astonishment and disbelief kept their minds elsewhere. They cruised along East Town streets piecing together the story they had just been handed. Ducci was a mentor of sorts. He gave them their start. Ducci held only one thing higher than loyalty and that was family.

"Where are we going to now?" John said from the passenger's seat. His gaze blurred shortly past the window.

"To see Marty." Luis said with clarity his brother lacked. "He knows more than he was letting on."

CHAPTER NINE

THE lights were off. The sound of water trickled from multiple small battery generated waterfalls. A land line rang. A second ring clattered. King Lito inhaled deep on his cigar, igniting the tobacco sending a red glow around his face, creating blackened eyes twice their normal size. He dropped his hand on the receiver, "Uhuh....Si......and the brothers left there in a hurry. So he failed. Did they have the case?....Find the case then kill them both."

Pressure built in Lito's head. It was not the incoming tropical depression rolling in saturated clouds. Headache medicine would not relieve this ache. Calls had come in, calls Lito did not want to have to answer but could not avoid. The Mafia bosses back in Mexico City wanted to be updated. They wanted to know where their money had gone. Lito had answers, too many answers and that was the problem. The bosses wanted one answer, the correct answer, that he had the device and was sending it on to Mexico City.

Sweat beaded across Lito's creased forehead. He had not moved from his office chair in hours. Water continued to trickle creating what were supposed to be soothing sounds. The type on the box said the tropical sounds reduced stress. Twelve waterfalls had not helped. Working with the lowest of low thugs willing to double cross the second biggest boss in town was now seen as a mistake. Rico had not lived up to his street credit. If the Collectors had not killed him, Lito's men would.

Lito pulled another cigar. A hand came across his face with an open flame. He puffed then waved the hand off. Hector withdrew the lighter placing it in his pocket. He was Lito's right hand man when it came to clerical issues, such as ordering murders and lining up lawyers for legal issues. Through all that, this was the most stressed he had seen his boss.

Lito ran yet another hand through his thick black hair turning the straight hairs wavy and the wavy hairs curly. His hand came off the top of his scalp. Lito got out of his chair to pace as he puffed away another cigar.

"The bosses want their money back." He mumbled to no one but himself. Then he said in Spanish, "Those damn brothers...I was on my way out, on my way out! No more bosses no more of their shit!" He looked to his loyal solider with the lighter, "Kill this guy, kill that one." He sat back in his former seat of power, now it was nothing more than a fly trap. The large leather arms and plush back gripped his wide frame tightly. Lito threw the cigar and rose back to his feet. Hector shifted his weight, unsure of how to react. His notorious boss was coming apart in front of him. Lito looked to him, waiting on an answer. His silence fueled Lito's rage.

"If those two shit poor excuses for collectors cost me going legit and getting out of this ball busting mafia....I'm gonna peel off their skin and make piñatas out of it. I'll laugh as the little ninos whack at them with their sticks and bust open their guts."

Hector smiled, hoping it would calm his boss. It only disgusted Lito. "Get out of my sight. Get out there and kill those brothers." He pounded his fist against the thick oak desk until Hector scurried out.

After two days of constant ringing, the phones were silent. Only trickling water now called to Lito. Sand in Lito's hourglass had reached the final grains. It would not be long now and so Lito sat at his desk listening to the trickling water from tiny waterfalls made someplace in China. Then came a thud from somewhere out in the flower shop. Lito watched as the brass knob on his office door began to rotate. Light cut a slice out of the dark room. The round boss made no movement or sound. He sat as if his oldest friend were about to enter. And he did.

Jose Diaz led with a half step into the room. His lean silhouette cast a scarecrow shadow across the room. Lito chewed what was left of his cigar, breaking the leaves apart in his mouth, wet leaves stuck to his lips.

"Hola Jose." Lito picked at the chewed end of the rolled tobacco leaves. He snubbed the rest in the ashtray.

"Hola Juan Miguel." Jose held a nickel plated Berretta. The mother of pearl handle inlay was a gift from Lito when the Mafia granted them control of the Juarez province. The pistol, engraved with a Mexican Flag, was part of a set. The other hung from a shoulder holster on a hall tree across the room.

"Which of my men have you killed out there Jose?" Lito picked up a pen and scribbled on a tablet.

Jose shrugged his shoulders, "I don't know Lito, I saw many new faces." The pistol remained leveled at Lito.

Lito scribbled down that all of his men in the building were presumed dead. Bushy black eyebrows pushed up into a rippled forehead. "And me Jose?"

Jose nodded. The once best friends had gone separate ways after Juarez was taken away from them. Though they both remained working for the Mafia, Lito came to the States to run a small syndicate for the Mafia while Jose stayed on the boarder perfecting his trade of death. The two men met again, both older and wiser with years of experience in the business. It was not the meeting they wanted but since the bad business deal with Tony Wren it was expected.

Lito's round body moved faster than a man of his age and size should. He ducked beneath the large desk as two nine millimeter rounds thudded against the thick oak. A quick boom thundered from the front of the desk and the two chairs opposite splintered as buck shot ripped through them.

99

Splinters flew through the air, Jose spun and covered his face from the wooden shrapnel. A second boom sent more shot down the middle. The second blast was no threat to Jose, but he took cover behind the door jam anyway.

From his hands and knees Lito shouted, "I tripped the alarm Jose. My men are coming."

"Why tell me?"

"Leave now amigo, never come back and you will have your life."

"Juan Miguel, I have come to kill you. There is no place for me to go." Jose's skinny arm pointed the pistol around the corner. He fired two quick shots blindly in to the room. It was enough for Lito to snatch his hand from the top drawer leaving the thirty-eight.

Lito danced his hand back into the drawer coming up with the snub nose this time. "Have it your way amigo." He stretched his arm over the desk and fired two shots into the door jam. One passed through nearly missing Jose, forcing him to retreat down the hall.

A round head popped up from behind the desk. Two black eyes peered around the room searching for any movement. The only thing moving was the image on the security monitor. Lito watched as the scarecrow figure ran through the dark flower shop, careful to stop at the end of each isle before proceeding to the next. A bell chimed as the man exited. The upper left monitor showed the front of the shop. A black SUV skidded to a stop. Two tinted windows zipped down as machineguns pointed out.

The scarecrow hopped like a marionette as the pinhead flashes of fire appeared at the end of each machinegun. The shooting stopped and two men jumped out, snatched the body from the gutter and tossed it in the back of the SUV.

Lito's phone rang again. "Ahlo."

"Jeffe, are you okay?" said the out of breath voice presumably from the SUV.

"Yes it is over. Dump the body and keep after the Collectors."

"Si, si." Lito watched the SUV speed off.

CHAPTER TEN

"REMEMBER that crazy Scottish family, the MacNaughtons?" the memory put a smile on John's worn face.

"Yeah, and that family photo, me in a family of redheads. Man, the parents would booze it up and then take it out on us."

John frowned again. "I can't believe the state would let children into a home like that. And that girl of theirs that was always sneaking into your bed. You'd say 'No we're brother and sister'. She'd say 'Not really'." The smile returned. John slapped his brother's shoulder.

"Maybe if she had been hotter. What a bunch of inbreeds."

"Even then you could always get the girls." John's reminiscing was cut short as the Cadillac was bumped from behind. "What the hell Luis?" The Cadillac was bumped again.

"Wasn't me bro." Luis glanced up at the rearview mirror. A black Lincoln swerved back and forth taunting the driver of the Cadillac. "This guy doesn't know who he is dealing with." Luis cut the steering wheel to the right and hit the brakes. The Cadillac laid black rubber as the Lincoln passed. All eight cylinders fired as Luis gunned the motor. This time the Cadillac bumper tapped the rear of the Lincoln. Bobbing and swerving, both cars raced through the empty East Town streets. They scraped paint and rubbed doors.

Luis clenched his teeth as he fought the wheel for control the car.

"Lose this guy already." John said with one hand on the door and the other bolted to the dash.

"This guy is a professional." Luis cut the wheel again as the tires screamed out. John looked out his window at the competing car. The tint on the Lincoln windows made it difficult to see the driver. A large silhouette appeared over the roof from the passenger's side of the Lincoln. The familiar shape of a MP 5 finished off the silhouette. The gun belched fire and spit lead.

John's window shattered raining glass down on the brothers. Luis cut the wheel sharply peeling away from the Lincoln. Rounds continued to rip at the steel of the Cadillac. Luis cut back into the Cadillac brining it too close for the shooter to get a good angle down. A few random shots spark off the pearl Cadillac.

John pulled his pistol and fired two rounds into the driver's window of Lincoln. Each round hit the tinted window fracturing the glass into two spider webs but did not shatter the window.

The Lincoln pulled away. The driver's side window of the Lincoln rolled down. The driver leaned back as the barrel of the MP5 stuck out.

Fire and crash sent bullets into and over the hood of the Cadillac. John watched them impact the hood of the Cadillac. Wind rushed into the car drowning out the roar of the engine. Taking all that fire, Luis chose to bail. He turned the wheel hard left, sending the car into a skid. John had a moment of clarity as he leveled his .45 and leaned forward through the passenger window against the force of the retreating Cadillac. A squeeze of the trigger fired three rounds at the now perpendicular Lincoln.

The Lincoln spun ninety degrees hitting a light pole, bounced back completing a 180 and wedged under a parked sod truck.

Luis wheeled the Cadillac slowly to the mashed up Lincoln beneath the sod truck. They left the Cadillac and ran with pistols out. John got out first and headed for the passenger's side. The door was crumpled down and the rood peeled back like a can of tuna. Inside White sat bleeding from the head. One lens from his amber sun glasses was gone, the other cracked. The eyes beneath circled the drain. His breath was shallow. One of his long legs was bent obtusely at the knee. The driver's side was crushed under the truck trailer. John pulled the door open. A head rolled out and onto the street. John recoiled in disgust. Luis looked down at a pair of empty eyes looking back.

"Looks like Logan's man Rolind."

John stood on the other side of the car. With one hand on the door and the other holding a pistol he said, "Looks like another one of Boss Ducci's hired killers, automatic weapons and all. Ducci's hiring some big guns to see us dead."

Luis came around to see for himself. "I know this one. Met him up north on a job. His name is White and he doesn't come cheap."

"Or doesn't come at all."

Police sirens crept into their ears as squad cars approach from far away.

"Come on we're taking him with us."

They dragged the six and half foot White to the rear of the Cadillac. They heaved White headfirst into the trunk. White grunted but did not struggle as he was crammed into a space too small for his frame. The brothers struggled with the hitman's lower half. John twisted the bent leg getting it to go. John slammed the lid down on White's protruding leg a few times but the lid would not close.

"This guy is huge. Unless you have a saw to cut his legs off, I don't think he'll fit."

"I've got something." Together they lifted White out. John balanced the man against the car while Luis dug around in the trunk.

"Dude, I wasn't serious about the saw."

Luis came up with a pair of bungee cords. "This will hold the lid down."

They stuffed White in the trunk, jamming his knees down once more. Luis strapped the bungee cord to keep the lid down, but White's knees protrude. It would have to do. Police sirens sounded only blocks away. The brothers needed a safe place to lay low and to question their captive.

A strip mall somewhere south on US 1 sat tucked back between two larger and better maintained shopping centers lined with higher end stores. This strip was painted a faded lime green. All the signs above each shop (only three of the eight store fronts were occupied) were painted with a white back ground and black letters naming the store. On the end was "Butcher" and beneath it, "Carnecia". The lights were off in the front but a dim orange glimmer from the rear directed Luis that way.

John hopped out of the idling wrinkled up Cadillac and walked to the screen door of the carnecia. Inside a round faced Hispanic man with a long pointed goatee dropped a cleaver down decisively into some fatty pink meat. John rapped on the door. The man stopped mid swing and turned slowly toward the door. His expression did not change as he neared the door.

The butcher stood in the doorway with an apron stained in every color red on the wheel. John held up a green and red chip, five hundred dollars. When the butcher opened the screen door a fly flew out, buzzing past John's face. The butcher held the chip in his palm for a moment then bit the corner and looked again. He grunted with a nod and took off the apron. Underneath the man was clad in a skintight wrestling singlet. The singlet was black spandex with neon green stripes down each side.

Dropping the apron in John's hands the butcher said, "Make sure and lock up. This is a rough neighborhood." The butcher went to an overhead cabinet and retrieved an open faced helmet and keys. He paused at the open screen door and said, "You should check out my show. It's Saturday night at the Ocean Arena.   Bring your friends." He smiled revealing he did not have all his teeth. A few yards away was parked a Harley and the butcher and part-time amateur wrestler mounted up and rode off.

John stood holding the apron. It dawned on him he held a smile on his face and a blood stained apron in his hands. He shook it off and waved Luis over who was waiting at the back of the Caddy with the trunk lid up.

Inside the shop, one low watt bulb struggled to keep the filament lit. In the center of the floor to ceiling ceramic tiled room was a four by eight butcher-block table. Deep gashes and slices in the pale yellow wood had once run over with blood leaving them a permanent rust colored stain.

They spread White out on a huge butcher-block table, stained in swatches of crimson. At each corner are black nylon tie downs. On one end, Luis slipped through a pair of wrists as John does the same with a pair of ankles. Blue veins pop as White struggled against the restraints. Luis paced back and forth, putting on stained leather gloves and mashing busy hands together. He converted the nervous anxiety into repeated blows to White. White was unfazed, it was nothing more than a scratch to be itched.

John loomed in the shadows, "We know you contracted out with Logan Ducci."

"The severed head in your lap," Luis growled, "that was his driver Rolind. Logan must be offering a lot to get you out of Seattle."

White remained silent. Luis stepped over to a peg board displaying multiple knives of different shapes and sizes. He ran his hand over several, taking in the size, shape and brand. Luis grabbed a curved blade and stood over White. The blade ran along White's shirt cutting it open. White's exposed chest was covered in scars ranging from a spider web to slashes and puffy stab wounds.

White picked his head off the table, "This is nothing new to me Luis. Do your best." He laid it back and took a deep breath. Luis twisted the blade midway between White's ribcage and his pelvis. He did not apply much pressure, just enough to draw blood. White laughed as though he were tickled.

John stepped into the light from the lone bulb above. He held a small yellow container with the graphic of a red flame and in the other hand an open Zippo. "We want answers from you White."

White remained silent. He was unfazed by the threats. John squeezed lighter fluid from the container into White's wound. White struggled hard now. John dragged the Zippo over his thigh and came up with a flame. John touched the flame off. White's side sizzled burning blue. White screamed and pulled against the zip ties. White quieted as the blue flame dissipated. John poured more fluid onto White this time down his bare arms. Again, the flame lit up. White screamed.

"I'll tell you! Put me out, put me out!" White shouted as the fluid burned ever closer to his neck and face.

Luis pulled a Clorox bottle out from under the sink and flipped the cap off. He dumped the bleach on White. White screamed again as the flames were extinguished.

The flames died out as the room filled with the stench of burnt flesh. "Boss Ducci hired me to come after you and take both your heads. Five hundred grand a piece." White said through gritted teeth.

"That's it?" John looked to Luis. They shared disappointment in White's limited response.

White a forced rhythmic breathing that calmed his nerves and allowed him to manage the pain. "Oh, I am sorry. Did I disappoint you with my simplistic answer to your unsophisticated questions?"

"Well, something a little more in depth would be nice."

"Yeah." John added.

"So would you prefer my confessions in 16th Century English prose, perhaps I should center my Chie and ask 'What would Confucius do?' Really, you two over complicate things." White coughed and spit pink out of the corner of his mouth. "Is it not enough that I have to go through life as a six foot six Albino suffering from alopecia, whose only occupation is killing? Now you want me to spout age-old philosophical rhetoric to help explain away your pathetic existences. I'm a contract killer, as simple as that."

John threw half a leg over a stool. "Five hundred a piece?" He set the lighter fluid on the counter. "So we're worth a total of a million. I'm not sure how I feel about that Luis. I thought in this day and age two high-class collectors such as us would go for a higher price."

Luis leaned against the wall. He proceeded as though White was no longer in the room. "I guess Ducci doesn't think as highly of us as we do. If he is willing to pay a million to see us dead than its going to cost him that and more." Luis smiled, satisfied with the amount of money on his head.

"Ducci must have really bought Rico's story to hire this freak to come after us? I thought we were good with Ducci. All the money we collected for him over the years should account for something."

"Yeah and that something's changed." Luis tugged at his stained leather gloves. "We must have fucked up somewhere. We know how Ducci works - he won't stop with just hearing that we are dead." Luis pointed to White strapped to the table, "This is just the beginning of the gamut we're about to run." Luis threw a punch at White's head out of frustration.

White blinked staring up at the dim bulb. "You two really don't know." A smile crinkled the corners of his bloody mouth. Blood trickled down one corner. "The Collectors running around untouched, getting away with everything and getting a pass from everyone - never tied to any mob or gang, no allegiances." The reputation of John and Luis Solo carried resentment and a jealously that would never be admitted. White left the rainy North West for the opportunity to put a bullet in each of the two collectors.

"You're an independent same as us."

"I never shit were I eat," White shook his head. He had taken this job for several reasons and one of them was that East Town was about as far from Washington State as he could get. The other reason was his belief that it would be over quickly. This abduction and interrogation was just a blip in his process. He believed it would be over soon. "You killed somebody important to him, a family member or something. Ducci is paying by the minute to ensure a slow death for you two *rookies*."

Luis and John locked eyes, Luis raised an eyebrow. Moving at light speed they grabbed White moving in separate directions but as one. John pulled a boot knife and cut the ties restraining White's left hand. Luis gripped White by the wrist and shoved it in the meat grinder. White struggled letting out a roar, Luis used all his strength to hold White in the grinder. John sprang on the grinder and began to crank the arm. White screamed then went limp.

To no one's surprise the sun rose in the east. The brothers had driven the night away, cruising the East Town streets, hoping the distraction of the drive would spring forth ideas on getting out of their predicament. With the new dawn came hunger. The Cadillac was backed into a spot near the dumpster of a chromed out diner. The street lamps above began blinking off as their timer expired with the end of night. Through the window of the diner John and Luis sat, heavy in thought but neither was showing. John shoveled the skillet platter breakfast filling his cheeks. Luis sipped coffee, tiny slurps that ensured his cup would last until the waitress returned.

John paused his chewing onslaught to sip badly needed water. Luis jumped in, "What's the plan?" He said finally putting the coffee mug down.

John gulped his water then said, "I was hoping you would have one." He shoveled another fork full of hash and eggs into his mouth.

Luis shook his head and looked down at the empty coffee mug. John dropped his fork and pushed his plate away. He said with his mouth full, "First we call in back up. Then we make our way home to the Palm."

"Going back to the Palm is suicide. That place will be crawling with bounty killers. We're to be killed by the minute remember." Luis slid the mug between his hands like a puck on the ice. "Damn it, it sounded like such a neat and easy job, one case, fifty grand. What a mess. Now we're stuck between two psychos.

If we call in back up things could literally blow up in our faces."

"White is one of the best hired killers in the country and we took him out. I don't know if we just got lucky or if it was skill, but I'm not willing to test that again, not without help."

Luis looked up from an untouched meal of eggs and hash. The eggs had been ordered over easy but came to him a runny bile mess. John had food on his chin. Luis stared annoyed with the food on John's chin that he refused to wipe.

"You know what bothers me in movies?"

John's eyebrows rose, confused by Luis' off candor question.

"I hate it when in movies an actor is eating and gets food on their face. If the food is not wiped off right away, I have to ask myself 'Did the director purposely pose the food there?' I mean, was there take after take to get that dribble just right? Or was it all a mistake and the scene was just so good he left it?" Luis tossed John a napkin. John wiped his chin.

"If the director does tell the actor to eat sloppy," John said, following his brother's train of thought, "then the question is why?"

"Why what?" Luis fired back, pushing his brother to a conclusion he was only began to draw.

"Why be sloppy, why be neat? Look, Rico kills Tony but leaves the case. Sloppy or neat?"

Luis pushed raw egg around his plate before taking a mouth full. There were just too many questions.

They had interrogated two of the best East Town's underworld could produce and they were not much closer to why a bounty was placed on their heads. Loyalty to Ducci left them wearing blinders.

"Rico was sloppy. The gambling device was not supposed to be left in the motel room for us; we were supposed to get a case with cash in it."

"Sloppy or not the men after us are dead serious. We're gonna need backup if we're going to war. I think it's time to make the call." John regained his appetite enough to finish off his plate. Luis put his fork down and reached for his cell. He speed dialed a number.

A low voice answered on the other end, "Quien es?" The voice filled his lungs with tobacco. The sound of traffic and sirens in the back ground filled the seconds of silence.

"Hey man it's me. We need your expertise for a bad collection. Oh, and bring your tool box."

The rasp of smoke leaving tar filled lungs blew over the other end of the cell phone. "Uh huh." The line went dead. Luis slid the cell phone into his coat pocket.

"Backup is on its way." Luis grinned and took another bite of food.

In an unknown location to the collector brothers, a man lay on a single bed. A fan spun slowly up above him. On his chest sat an ashtray filled with the day's ash. His skin was a rutty yellow and his hair black, pulled tightly into a ponytail. His cheek bones pushed high and wide with sparse black hair forming a mustache between them. He snubbed out the cigarette and rolled off the bed.

On one knee he reached under the bed and pulled foot locker. Inside the locker were the tools of death. Several different handguns, ranging from twenty-two to forty-five caliber, covered the top of the mound in the locker. Each handgun was in a sealed Ziploc bag. The man sifted through his inventory, plucking the weapons he believed he would need.

CHAPTER ELEVEN

THE decision was not to go to the lion's den but where they will all be hanging out. Starved and bored the lions paced around the lobby of the Beach Palm Hotel. When the jalopy that used to be Luis' prized and polished Cadillac limped into the employee parking lot two lions sat in a van sharpening their teeth.

Luis circled the battled GM around the lot. "What's the plan boss? You won't get ten feet into the hotel before being cut to pieces or worse. Real good idea coming home, John." He kept his eyes scanning and a pistol on his lap.

"I got it under control." John bounced out of the car.

A few parking spaces down a young Beach Palm employee was parking his Ford Maverick, ready to start his shift. John appeared, filling the driver's side window. The window was down and Chaddick was just shutting off the engine.

"I'm gonna need your clothes Chaddick."

Chaddick was slow to look up. "Uh? Oh hey Mr. Solo, what was that?" Chaddick's young eyes went round as he looked up to John Solo, leaning in over the car door. Chaddick had watched the Collectors for the last year of his employment at the Beach Palm leave the hotel fresh and clean then return a day or two later worn but dropping lots of cash. He wanted that life style for himself, something that would give him a story while bellied up at the bar.

"No time to explain, get undressed." John began to unbutton his shirt. Chaddick looked up confused. This was not the way he had dreamed of helping out the Collectors. In his mind it would go down with John or Luis coming into the hotel asking questions only Chaddick would know the answer to. Then they would tell the hotel front desk manager that they had to take him with them. Chaddick would head out with the Collectors on an awesome adventure. But not like this.

"Come on get your pants off. I need your uniform. Let's go, get it off." John snapped his fingers, he was already shirtless. Chaddick got out of the crappy little car and immediately began to undress.

"Oh, I get it. You guys are after someone." Chaddick pulled his black polo shirt up over his head. "No wait... some one's after you. Yeah and you need my clothes..." Chaddick handed over his red vest to John.

"Yeah something like that. You got a hat back there?"

Shirtless, Chaddick turned and dove into the back seat of his beater ride. From the back seat he said, "Oh yeah I got a hat here somewhere. Man, helping the Solo brothers. Dude, Ryan's never going to believe me." When he would retell this story to his friend it would not be his clothes he turned over.

Chaddick popped up with a Cleveland Indians Baseball cap.

"Pants too." John had his jeans down around his ankles. Chaddick dropped his pants. John tugged them up, leaving the button undone.

"How do I look?" John turned in a circle. Skipping an answer he said, "Listen, chances are when I come out of the hotel guys with guns will be trying to kill me. So here," John flipped Chaddick a hundred dollar green and white chip. "I hope this covers it."

Chaddick had proof for his story.

John walked off in a bellman uniform a size too small. The outline of a forty-five automatic jutted from his waist band.

Chaddick looked back as John Solo left in his uniform. "Yeah sure Mr. Solo. No worries, you can keep it as long as you need." Chaddick stood in his boxers. He rubbed the chip between his fingers and felt a smile break across his face.

John walked with careful attention to the men in oversized sport coats loitering around the hotel entrance. Ducci's crew all looked the same, there was the man about fifty with a goatee that was more grey than black. His sunglasses looked cheap like they were bought in a hurry at a convenience store. He wore a polo shirt under a sport coat cut broad at the shoulders and stayed wide to the waste in an attempt to hide the pistol beneath. There were more like him parked in cars or walking, wondering about.

The one coming through the doors held his hand at his waste. His fingers were fanned with his thumb resting on his belt. He stopped cold as John slowed his pace.

John kept his eyes below the brim of the cap. He spotted a plump woman in a purple blouse and matching polyester pants getting out of a taxi. The newest bellman at the Beach Palm raced to grab her one suitcase.

"Hey you." The plump plum spat through wrinkled smokers lips. "I can carry my own luggage thank you." She reached for the handle but John was faster. "Okay, but don't expect a tip. Remember I didn't ask you to carry that. Now I'm on the third floor room, um, room." The woman ducked her head into her enormous arm bag in search of her room key. The pair passed through the double doors past the hood with the trigger finger. Convinced John was a bellman the hired gun continued out of the hotel.

Once in the lobby John headed for the front desk. The hotel guest told him her room was the other way. John dropped the luggage.

"Third floor? Not without a tip! Carry it yourself."

The Front Desk Manager, Jason, caught the disturbance early. This was his hotel lobby and no disturbance would go unnoticed. Jason was early thirties, black hair shaved tight, and dressed in a suit that took time to make. His nametag was shiny and his shoes polished. He stood behind the check-in desk with a balled fist on the desktop.

"Ah Chaddick, can I see you in my office?" Jason said with concern in his voice. John moved toward the side office door leaving the guest bewildered and frustrated.

Jason held the side door open as John passed Jason said, "Outside of work we are great friends. At work you two drive me fucking nuts."

John went through with his head down low and a grin on his face. Jason looked John up and down dressed in the tight bellman uniform. "I would fire you, coming to work dressed like that."

Jason did not say a word. He walked with John in tow down a hall back to his office. At the office door he paused, over his shoulder he said, "You know *she* wants to see you two." He pushed his key into the lock and they entered.

"I'm sure Morgan just wants to see Luis. She can't stand me."

The office was small and windowless. A wood laminate desk separated the two. Jason remained standing as he looked John up and down dressed in the tight bellman uniform. "Mrs. Dennis would fire me if she caught one of my bellmen dressed like that."

Jason turned to a framed print entitled "Vivid Chintz". The print resembled some sort of plant life on a red silkscreen background. Jason's mouth opened but no words came out. He slide the picture aside and punched a pass code into the wall safe.

"I thought one of you would be stopping by for this case. Judging by the goons that have been loitering out in the parking lot since last night, I'd say you guys are in trouble. I had Nancy transfer the briefcase from the guest safe to my private one here." Jason put the case down on his desk. John snatched it up.

"Thanks Jason, I-"

Jason shook his head, "No need. It's probably best I don't know what's going on. As much grief as you brothers bring to my hotel I like having you around, don't ask me why, but I do."

John looked his tolerating friend in the eye, "All right Jason, fair enough. You know you can always come with us." John's words hung in the air then he said, "You mind letting me use the back door to this place?"

"Yeah you can use the celebrity exit. I'll need to unlock it for you." Jason closed up the safe and lead John back down the hallway. They crossed the lobby and past the elevators, picking up a tail. John changed the handle of the case from his right to left. Jason eyed the older men in cheap sport coats and accelerated his pace. The pair took the stairs to the third floor. Once in the stairwell, John leaned over the rail to see the tail attempt to flatten against the stairwell wall. Through the third floor door and half way down the hall, John followed Jason.

Beside each door on the third floor was a brass plate engraved with a room number. Halfway down the hall the pair stopped at a door with no mark. Jason dug in his pants pocket for a ring of keys. As he slipped a key into the lock a man in a sport coat stepped out from the vending machine cove.

The man raised a pistol and fired. The bullet ricocheted off the steal case. Jason pushed against the locked door. The man in the sport coat advanced. John slipped his forty-five out and fired one round into the man's neck. The forceful round snapped the man's head nearly coming off, knocking him to the ground.

From behind John's left came a knife wielding bounty killer. He struck downward with the serrated blade. Again, the case acted as defense glancing the man's blow. John shoved the barrel in the man's chest but before he could squeeze the man swatted it away with one hand and swung the other. John leaned back but not enough. The blade sliced open the bellman polo along with the top layer of John's skin.

The pain did not register for John. He straightened up and brought his left arm up, swinging the case down on top of the bounty killer's head. With a thud, the case conformed to the shape of the man's crown. His eyes rolled white as his body imploded.

John felt a tug on his right. He swung his pistol and buried it deep into Jason's belly. Jason's eyes went wide. His face shouted for John not to pull the trigger.

John relaxed his grip. He tucked the pistol in his pants and went through the door.

Once on the other side Jason said whipping sweat beads from his brow, "Damn it John." A smile began to creep at the corners. He fought hard but lost. "Get the hell out of here."

"Thanks Jason. I owe you."

"You owe me a fucking lot." Jason said with a slight nudge to his friend.

John slipped through the celebrity exit, an unmarked door on the third floor of the parking garage. Luis hit the ignition on the Caddy and dropped the tranny into drive. The tires screamed out as Luis wheeled the car through the tight turns of the parking garage. He locked the brakes just in time to see John come barreling out of an unmarked door with no handle. He held the case high and fanned his arms for Luis to get the Caddy ready to roll.

From behind a pillar a curly haired man in a track suit raised a pistol too big for him to handle. He fired once losing his balance, causing him to stumble to the ground. As he was getting to his feet a second man trailed out the celebrity door. This man, similarly dressed, pushed his counterpart back to the ground as he paused to take aim at John.

John sprinted toward the running car. He locked eyes with Luis who had drawn his pistol and leveled it right at John. John slid along the smooth concrete floor as if to slide for second base. With the scent of blood in the air the lions began to circle. A spray of bullets peppered the side of the Cadillac. Luis opened his door with his left hand while firing two more rounds from the right. A grunt came from the shadows of the parking garage.

Luis double gripped his pistol and stepped forward. Two men lay bleeding and dying. Luis stood in the silence of the parking garage. John extended out of the rear window with a pistol pointed out and said, "Do we have time to stop off for a decent shirt?"

John and Luis sat on a low brick lined wall on top of a three story building just off Beach Street overlooking the old downtown. With the sun to their backs, they sat drinking sweating beers. John stood and finished the last foamy drops of his beer. He looked out at the inner coastal river and beyond to the tall concrete canyon lining the strip of the beachside peninsula.

They had spent nearly their entire lives crisscrossing every street in the neon infested streets of East Town. From his vantage point John could point out where he first drove a car. A foster dad passed out leaving the keys to his 1966 Olds 442 lying out. It was all young John needed to expel the pent up testosterone a fourteen year old has. The cops picked him up over there off Peninsula Drive peeling out of a 7 Eleven. The memories continued to flash of a misspent youth. Truth chiseled at the back of his skull, it was time to leave.

"Come and get us you sons of bitches!" John shouted and threw his bottle off the roof. The green glass projectile crashed into the remains of a vacant lot now reclaimed by nature and people looking to dump old furniture.

"I'm getting real sick of this game." John continued, "We're gonna need to kill all of those bastards if we're to get out of the middle of this mess." He flung his arms apart feeling the sting of the cut he received earlier by one of the bounty killers. The brothers had to face their accusers or run and if they ran they could never come home again.

Luis sipped his beer then said, "Maybe in the middle is where we want to be."

"Right now it's like we're a couple of mice caught between two cats and they're just toying with us, taking their time with the kill. As soon as we poke our heads out of the mouse hole we're dead. I don't want to just sit around waiting to die."

Luis continued with his calm demeanor. "No, no that wont work for me either." Luis finished his beer and wiped his mouth. His gaze traveled out over the water and the gambling skyline. "The problem is right now Ducci and Lito are unknowingly working together, for the same cause, to kill us, right. We need them to be fighting each other instead. Pin them against each other while we make our escape."

"How do we get them to turn on each other like that? What do we have to offer?"

"I know how, but first we're gonna need bait and we're gonna need guns."

"Good, I've been looking do some more killing."

CHAPTER TWELEVE

AT night a pair of legs dangling from a trunk lid would not attract much attention. During the day it was a different story.

Luis looked up into the rearview mirror. Blue and red lights flashed in a circular motion. "Shit."

John flipped in his seat for a view out the rear window. "Damn, five-O. Really, how long did we think driving around with a six foot six killer hanging out of the trunk would go unnoticed?" John pulled his .45 from his waistband, thumbing back the hammer.

Luis sucked his teeth. "Be cool brother." He said without looking at John. "Half the cops in this town are on the take or smack junkies. Try pulling some green instead of lead and maybe we can get out of this one alive." John put the .45 away. Luis pulled to the shoulder, the cop followed behind them.

Officer Hagerty sat in his squad car running the plates of the Cadillac. His monitor popped up a registration to the Beach Palm Casino Hotel and clean. He looked up at the pair of knees protruding from the bungeed trunk lid. Grabbing the microphone he said over the megaphone, "Okay you two, I want to see four hands dangling from the window."

The Brothers complied, dangling their hands out of the window.

"Now slowly get out of the car. Walk with your hands on the car towards me." Hagerty opened his door and placed a hand over the grip of his pistol.

Again the Brothers complied. They exited the car palms pressed along the car until they were standing at the rear.

Hagerty approached them with his gun drawn. He was a stout black man with wide eyes and a thin mustache. "Well damn John, Luis. How the hell are you?" The pistol went back into its leather container. "I ran your plate but the car came back registered to the Palm Casino. If I had known it was you two I'd..." Hagerty extended his hand to shake with the brothers.

Luis used caution as he said, "Officer Hagerty, nice to see you."

"Yeah, it's been awhile hasn't it? What have you two been up to?" Hagerty rested a hand on the trunk as the brothers looked on with worry.

"The usual stuff." John replied. Hagerty looked at both brothers waiting for more of a story. When they did not comply he filled the silence, "A car matching this one was reported leaving the scene of an accident early this morning. You two wouldn't know anything about that would you?" Hagerty surveyed the damage on the car. John and Luis step apart in preparation to jump Hagerty if they had to. Hagerty bent down and peeked into the trunk. A man, bound and bleeding, stared back at him.

"Well just who do we have here?"

Luis put a hand on the trunk.

John stepped around saying, "A crazed psychopathic hit man who has been running all over town trying to kill us."

Officer Hagerty paused; he put his hand back on his pistol, and then snapped the strap down. "Okay boys, just burry this one deep and leave no trace. Take him out to the swamps or someplace out of my jurisdiction." John and Luis relaxed with a smile.

Hagerty rubbed his dark brown eyes. "After what you two brothers did for me." The dark brown became surrounded by red. "The Misses…she'll never forget I tell you."

"That's what friends are for Hagerty." John patted Hagerty on the back.

"Yeah, real pals." Hagerty straightened up taking in a deep breath. "Okay boys I better send you on your way. I'll try and keep the fuzz off your tail concerning this…whatever it is you're mixed up in."

"Thanks Hagerty. Anything we can do for you."

"No, no Luis, it's on me, it's on me."

"Alright Hagerty, I'll remember you said that." The brothers got back in the beat up car. Hagerty stood, smiling, remembering how the brothers had bailed him out.

John climbed back into the front passenger seat as Luis got behind the wheel. "See, there's still one good cop in East Town."

CHAPTER THIRTEEN

THE Cadillac rolled down a neighborhood street. At a brown house in need of yard service, Marty and Cheryl sat on a motorcycle that Marty could not keep running. Marty looked up to see the familiar Cadillac. Marty gave Cheryl a shove off the bike. Marty twisted on the throttle and did his best with a wobbly take off. Luis swerved the Caddy as John jumped out running. Marty, being cut off, bailed. The motorcycle carried on a few more yards before spilling. John caught Marty by the collar and threw him into a dead bush below a window. Luis backed the Cadillac through the open garage.

Inside John shoved Marty into a worn chair like a child about to be punished. Luis made a sweep of the filthy house to be certain they would be alone with Marty. Together they stood over their one time friend.

The brothers stared silently at Marty. He shifted in his seat. "Who the hell is in the trunk? Whoever it is, I don't know him okay, I swear, right, I swear."

"The only time you're going to open that blabbering mouth of yours is when answering our questions. I don't want to hear your usual nonstop

131

bullshit running mouth or I'll just kill you here and get my answers somewhere else."

Marty nodded his reply. The door from the garage creaked open. Cherly walked in brushing dried grass off her expansive rear-end and looked up with an ugly face to see two forty-fives looking back.

Her expression did not change, "Marty? What's going on, who are these guys?" She continued into the room.

"Now Cheryl, I think you better go."

"But Marty I came here with you on the bike. My car's back at the bar. How the hell am I getting back?"

John reached into his pocket and pulled a chip. He flipped it towards the door she came in from saying, "Call a cab, and do it from outside."

"What! You call me a fucking cab!" Cheryl said through yellow teeth and crinkled lips.

John frowned. He looked back at her as he cocked the hammer of the pistol.

With two palms out Cheryl said, "Easy cowboy, this ain't high noon. I'm going." Complaining under her breath she bent over and picked up the chip.

Luis made a seat out of the coffee table across from Marty. He sat silent. John pulled a four inch boot knife and picked at dried blood under his fingernails.

The seconds ticked by. Marty spilled it. "This is gonna cast me in a bad light, right. Like, I've worked with you brothers along time. I ain't trying to go and mess that up. But I wrecked it bad this time. It was a lot of money for one phone call, right."

"Who told you to call us?" One brother said.

Marty wiped his moist upper lip. "Oh man he's gonna kill me. If you're here then he's gonna know I talked and"

"You don't think we won't kill you! Who paid you?" The other brother asked.

Looking down Marty braced for impact as he said, "Rico Sullivan, that's who." When nothing happened he opened one squinted eye, then the other to see John's smirk.

The smile turned to hard stone, "Don't worry about him. He's dead."

"Oh...good. That's all right with me."

"We weren't asking your permission. Now hurry up with your story before we toss you in the trunk with that bounty killer."

With a shaky hand, Marty grabbed a half-smoked cigarette from the ashtray along with a lighter. He inhaled deep. Smoke funneled out, "Okay. I'm at Spanky's Lounge and Games, right, having a few beers when Rico comes in. He's waving around big bills buying drinks, getting the girls all interested. The night goes on and I'm getting drunk by myself. This girl comes over and starts making conversation. Then she starts getting all touchy feely. I can't believe my luck. That's when Rico leans in and whispers his boss is interested in me for a job. I'm not paying attention because this half nude chick next to me starts rubbing hard on my crotch, right."

"Get to the freaking point. Who was his boss?"

"Yeah, so before I knew it I agreed to whatever he was saying. I don't know, all he ever said was 'boss' so I'm thinking Boss Ducci, right? We all love Boss Ducci, right? He took me out to his car, a bad ass El Camino, and hands me a couple of bricks of cash, covered in blue and red plastic wrap n' shit."

Luis cocked an eye brow up, "You mean like what flowers come wrapped in?"

Marty shrugged, "Yeah I guess, why?"

"King Lito." John said.

"Oh shit, oh shit, oh shit!" Marty tried to stand. John shoved him back down. "King Lito. I swear I didn't know Lito's fat ass was tied up in this. I never would take that Mexican blood money. Working for Lito is a death sentence." Marty put out his cigarette, Luis joined him in a new cigarette from his pack.

"So what were your orders from Rico?"

"Call you two and tell you where some guy named Tony Wren was staying at. Did you ever find him?"

Luis snubbed out his cigarette. "Dead. Same as Rico."

John finally took a seat in a blown out couch. "Yeah but we didn't kill him." His boots went up on the table.

"Guys, I swear I didn't know." Marty made eye contact for the first time without fear of receiving a blow. "The only two things you get working for Lito is tortured and dead. I never would have done what Rico told me to do if I knew who the orders were from."

John picked up a pen. Using a scrap paper wrapper he began to write something down. Without looking up he said, "I should be writing your suicide note. Then Luis will put a gun to your head and scatter your brains all over this room, but I'm not. Tell me, why all that coke?" John pointed with the pen to the open case of white powder. The coke had not moved since they paid their last visit to Marty's trashed house.

"Oh yeah that. Well..."

"That's gotta be worth more than Rico paid you. So where did all that come from Marty?"

John walked over and closed the case. "Yeah Marty, why all the coke?" Moving slowly, John dropped the case by Luis' feet. Marty's eyes followed the case. He wiped his lip once more.

"I'm thinking about dealing. I ...ah know a guy and he owed me some bucks on a Jai Alai game I fixed for him so I tell him to pay me in coke, right? See he's a direct importer and that's some pure shit. I cut it a dozen times, so I got a lot for a little. That junk is so watered down, nobody's getting high off it. It just looks good at parties right?"

Luis stood up with the case in hand. Marty's eyes dart, his hands twist. "Well Marty, now you owe us big." Luis headed for the door.

John laid down the note he scratched on the table, "Consider your debt paid."

Marty began to protest by standing, but knew standing could be met with physical violence. He sat.

"Hey my coke! Come on guys really it was nothing personal."

The brothers did not bother responding. Marty picked up the note and threw it back on the table. With his arms above his head, he said to an empty room, "And how the hell am I supposed to get a hold of Lito?"

The next step in Luis' plan required another stop to Roger's Go Navy, Beat Army surplus store. Inside the bell on the door did its job and alerted the young clerk that Luis and John had come in. The clerk, Kyle, in his late teens was wearing a Marine Corps battalion shirt two sizes too large and so were the pair of BDU pants he wore. He stood behind the counter. Luis walked to the counter and took off his sunglasses, laying them on the counter. John hung back choosing to loiter near the magazine rack. He flipped through Bunker monthly, voted best survivalist magazine the year before. The sign above the clerk's shoulder that read, "Cash or Credit only" below scribbled in Sharpie, a picture of a chip with a circle and line through it.

"You're new here, just out of Saint Gerard's?" Luis asked.

"Yeah, a few weeks now." Kyle's eyes skipped between the brothers.

"Good old St. Gerard, saint of the falsely accused. I guess Roger's taken you in. From one orphan who has survived it here to another, don't show fear the guy eats it for breakfast."

Kyle stared, unblinking at Luis. "Aahh. Should I get him for you?"

A voice from behind scraped over vocal cords abused by too much smoking said, "No need son, I'm coming." Footsteps of a man with a limp accompanied the voice. Roger appeared from the back. He was in his early sixties with white and left over blonde hair that was long and brushed to the side. His large frame emphasized his limp. A hand-cannon was strapped around his good leg. He held packages of MREs in his hand, a cane in the other. He took one look at Luis and placed the MREs randomly on a shelf.

"Que pasa Luis, John?" Roger's hand went out to Luis as he waved with the other to John.

"Nada Roger." Luis gave him a warm smile. The eighteen months Luis and John spent under Roger's foster was the best of their adolescent lives. Roger provided the warmth of someone who cared and combined it with the discipline all troubled youth lack.

John put down the magazine and hustled over to his brother's side. "We need to see some of your specialty items."

Roger looked to Kyle. Kyle maintained his blank stare.

"Kyle, why don't you sweep around the front and go ahead and lock up."

Kyle watched the sunshine forcing through the tinted glass of the storefront. "Ah sure I guess."

Roger turned and waved a hand to follow him back. Luis and John came around to the side of the counter. John grabbed a black duffle bag before following the man with the limp to the back of the store.

The trio stopped at a wall with homemade wooden shelves, the only shelves in the store not being maximized. Roger leaned his cane against the wall and said, "C'mear and give me a hand with this Luis."

The shelves slid to reveal a hung "DON'T TREAD ON ME" coiled snake flag. Roger pulled the flag back and raised a hand as if he were a doorman. The brothers stood with smiles on their faces and blood filling their hearts.

Stepping through, gun oil and stamped steel filled their noses. The room was a tight twelve by fifteen feet and lined floor to ceiling with armaments from around the world. The calibers ranged from twenty-two to fifty, some even coming in double-digit millimeter. In the center of the room was a green felt card table. John placed the bag on the table and opened it wide, eager to fill it. Roger leaned back with folded arms and showed off his gleaming white dentures as the boys he helped to mentor began to pick through his latest inventory.

Each rifle and pistol was inspected. An eye down the sights, slides pulled back, clips released, all for fun and all for preparation. John opened a crate and snatched up some flash bang grenades as well as shrapnel. Luis tossed in a couple of vests. He paused to look over a faded photo on the wall. A young Roger, limp free, stood with other sailors on the deck of a PBR (Patrol Boat, River). His shirt was off, as were the others and leaned against the deck gun, a fifty-caliber machinegun.

"How's the leg?" Luis said while continuing to sift through the weapons.

"Not as good as it was that day. Fucking V.C. You know the very next day is when I got blown off that deck. If it weren't for those villagers that found me in the marsh, I'd a been up shit creek... Come to think of it, we did call it Shit Creek." It was a story Roger recalled many times. Often it was at the request of his injured leg. The brothers knew it well, the story of Roger's two tours in Vietnam serving in the brown water Navy, picking up Navy Seals dropped behind enemy lines.

"What's new since last time?" John asked eager to handle something illegal. Roger pointed to Luis' left. On the wall was an AA-12, full auto shot gun.

"How about a street sweeper? Full auto twelve gauge. It fits a drum too. Watcha huntn'?"

"Men." Luis said taking the shotgun from the wall. His hands slide over every inch of the composite body.

Roger grunted. He grabbed a chair beside the small table. Before sitting he removed two unseen hand cannons and placed them on the table to make sitting more comfortable. "In packs or alone? If they're comin' in packs I'd suggest it."

Luis put the shotgun in the bag. "Just might be packs. I'll take that drum too. Oh and all these are clean right."

Roger's wrinkled eyes became narrow slits, "You have to ask? Here I thought you kept comin' around just to jabber jaw." His eyes went round again as a smile increased the wrinkles across his tanned face. Roger's smile faded. "No numbers no trace, barrels been swapped out too."

Luis put the street sweeper in the bag.

"Sounds like you boys got your selves in a pickle and shooting your way out is the answer."

"Yeah when the pickles are King Lito and Boss Ducci. I don't see any other way than that of the gun."

"Well I taught you two boys how to defend yourselves."

"That you did." Luis said adding a Taurus Judge to the bag.

"Don't worry Roger. We'll be careful."

"Hell, careful is a naked man climbing a barbed wire fence. You two were just a couple of tough looking boys who had never really been tested under fire when you come to me. Sure you were in and out of foster homes and had your fare share of school yard fights, but not like the ones you would be in, not like this one." Roger had seen many of Saint Gerard's boys pass under his roof. He tried his best with them all. Over the years there were still a few who came back. There was something different about John and Luis. Their bond never lessened over the years. It could have been the way they took to Roger's philosophies on life and death. It could have been a common spirit the three men seemed to share. Whatever it was, it was unbreakable.

"Sure Roger, you taught us about picking our battles. Knowing when to back down and when to stand and fight. We think this is the time to stand and fight." John zipped up the fully loaded duffle.

Roger stood and holstered his pistols. "Good, cause I also taught you to think for yourselves."

The three men stood at the counter. Luis set the weighted bag down with a clatter. Kyle peered curiously at the jabbing contours of the bag.

"I'll need four boxes of Federal APC .45, four boxes of 12 gauge, make that two shot and two slug, and that can of 5.56. How much?" Luis said to Kyle who had yet to remove his eyes from the bag. Having never been in the hidden room, he desperately wanted to know what was being sold.

"Oh and the bag." Luis added, patting the top of the bag.

Kyle punched buttons on the register. "Ah.. ninety-nine fifty."

Roger stood back; a smile wrinkled his face once more. A wad of cash tucked noticeably in his shirt pocket bulged. The Brothers shoved the ammo in exterior pockets of the bag, never opening the bag to expose the contents.

Hands were extended, "Via con Dios, Solo brothers."

CHAPTER FOURTEEN

MIKE sat along an empty highway lined on either side with low hanging oaks and gator infested canals. The layer of fat around his midsection strained the buttons on his white collared shirt. His suit pants were undone to make room for the day old meatball sub. The car radio played classic Italian music. It put Mike in the mood. The dispatch radio cracked, causing Mike to nearly lose a meatball.

"Mike. How's it lookin'?" the radio barked.

Through chewed meat, sauce and bread came the words, "Everything looks quiet. When am I getting relieved?" Another bite was stuffed before a swallow could make room.

"I told you we're spread thin. Ducci has guys all over town hunting those brothers. You come back when I tell ya! Out."

"Yea yea." Mike said without using the receiver. This was the bottom of Boss Ducci's barrel. All his good guys were out canvassing East Town looking to score the collection on the Solos. Those sitting the bench all this time were called up to play.

The music was too loud for Mike to hear the gravel crunch under the assassin's boots as they neared the parked car. Between chews, Mike opened his mouth

143

to sing along with his favorite part of the song. Just as his mouth opened to hit the high note, a black gloved hand jammed a black K-Bar through his throat, pinning his head to the head rest. He gurgled as un-chewed food fell from his open dying mouth.

Backup had arrived for the brother collectors. He lit a cigarette as he leaned against the car. He was dressed in an old snap up plaid western shirt and worn jeans finished out with worn boots. A dark bandana slung around his scalp holding back long straight black hair.

Later on up the road a car let off the accelerator and coasted to a stop a few yards away. The faces in the car were familiar. The pistol went back in its holster.

John was out of the car first. He leaned in Mike's window and said "What do we have here?" The blood that had gushed down the dead Ducci soldier's neck and chest was now dried rust.

"Looks like you've been here a while." John said pulling his head from the window.

"Backup has arrived." His eyes stared off down the road towards the Ducci compound. His face held no expression as he sucked the flame closer to his lips. Once he smoked the cigarette to the butt, he leaned in the window, turned on the ignition and dropped the gear shifter to drive. It took a shove to get the large sedan rolling. There was no splash as the car began to sink nose first into the brackish water.

"Good." Luis stepped forward and handed Backup a folded sheet of paper. "Head there and set up. We'll meet you at the designated time."

Backup shoved the paper in his back pocket. The three men walked to the back of the parked Caddy. White's dangling legs came alive with a jolt. John and Luis paid no attention to the imprisoned bounty killer. Backup watched the legs kick. He looked back at John who was in the backseat digging in a black duffle bag.

John came up wearing blue latex gloves and cradling a M4. He laid the M4 rifle on the roof and began loading a thirty round clip.

"I was up the road and saw the house. Nice compound you're up against."

"You know better than anyone it's always the hard way for us." John said with a smile. Backup's face remained stone.

Luis went around to the other side of the car. Before digging into the bag he said, "We don't run, we don't hide. This is going to be one hell of a fight. Neither side, Lito or Ducci, will ever back down or leave us alone. We have to do it this way."

"I will only ask once, you want me to come along?

"No," Luis came up from the back seat with the AA12. "We need some of them left alive and for the rest of the plan, you need to be in position."

"Once you start killing, don't stop until they're all dead." Backup flipped his cigarette into the canal and walked off down the road.

"You need a ride?"

Backup waved them off without turning around.

"Weirdo." John said under his breath.

"Yeah, but reliable."

The darkness of the trunk flooded with light as the lid lifted. White pinched his eyes to keep them from burning. Through narrow slits he looked up at John and Luis who stood with bullet proof vests on and carrying an M4 and the street sweeper.

"Ready for one last ride?"

White screamed from beneath the gag. The lid slammed to blackness.

The compound, a large riverfront home with large sloping arches in two tone stucco finished off with terracotta shingles, sat back off the road. Recently all the Spanish moss had been cleared from the low hanging oaks and flood lights were planted in the Saint Augustine grass. With an absence of men in ill fitting sport jackets and automatic weapons to guard the grounds, Ducci left it up to dogs.

On the second floor, two folding tables were paired end to end. On top monitors showed live images of the men in tracksuits walking around. Pacing and puffing, Ducci went back and forth watching the monitors, waiting for something to happen. More men dressed similarly lounged in overstuffed chairs. Their voices were low as they gabbed like the housewives they complained about.

"Boss we got a car coming in." said Nick, one of the last of Ducci's men left to guard the house. All the men in the house gathered around the monitors to watch a white battered Cadillac limp its way up the brick drive. The trunk lid bounced with every out of place brick.

"I don't believe it! Those Solos are dumber than I thought." Nick said turning to his boss.

"No, no that takes balls real big figgen balls." Ducci bit down on the end of his cigar severing the tip. "This otta be real damn good." Excitement forced drool from the corners of Ducci's smile.

Outside the Cadillac came to a stop. Barking Dobermans made their charge at the collectors. John unwrapped some graying steaks left in the back since their visit to the butcher's early this morning. The dogs focused their attention to the meat, taking it happily away to the reaches of the yard to be devoured. The brothers got out of the car with their plan succeeding so far.

At the back of the car, Luis hauled White from the trunk. The hitman had a hand wrapped and taped in butcher paper at the wrist. The paper was soaked through red with an indistinguishable odor as the meat. White has taken on a blue hue with a fever forcing sweat from every pore. His ruby eyes refuse to focus and his knees would not lock. Luis balanced White forcing him to move like a marionette. John came around and pressed a barrel to the base of White's skull. He shoved White forward. Luis strapped on the AA12.

The two collectors were suited up, armed and armored. They came to send a message, not from far or through a third person. They had worked with Ducci for a long time and felt he needed to see their faces when they delivered their final message. They owed him that.

"It's time."

Luis nodded then kicked open the door. They moved quickly.

Inside, the great front hall loomed large with two rising stairways on either far wall. It filled in quickly with eight to ten bad guys lining the walls and filling in door jams. Most had pistols or sub machineguns pointed at the brothers. Luis shoulder readied the AA12. John scrunched behind White to create less of a target. Ducci called from upstairs but remained hidden behind the wall.

"Do you bastards think you can trade your lives for that freak?"

"We just want a chance to settle this." Luis said through the side of his mouth as his face leaned near the stock of the shotgun. The barrel swept the room, hanging on one target after the other.

"You march into my house with guns out and you think that will settle it? You collectors had better rethink things. You killed my cousin, my blood. What am I going to tell his mother? She can't even have an open casket, say a proper goodbye thanks you two douches."

"You've been misinformed Ducci. We didn't kill him but we have something you might want. The case your cousin died for."

Ducci rubbed his chin. He had raised these two men to be collectors, the two men he now wanted dead. They have come to him with answers and all he has are guns. It did not matter, Tony was dead and they were mixed up in it. John and Luis had left the core principle of collecting behind; to leave your fish alive for another loan. It was time to sever ties permanently. "Finding out what you killed him for don't bring him back. Closure is watching your brains splatter all over my walls."

"We didn't kill Tony. We've come to offer you the truth." John now tried to reason. "If you want the real killers meet us at Colossal and Grand Street, two a.m. We can settle all this then."

The truth did not matter to Ducci. He motioned for two more men to move into the foray. They lock and load as they move, ready to shoot it out.

"We can settle it now." Ducci called in a taunting voice.

The gunmen enter with intent to kill. When outnumbered, open fire first. Luis opened with a short burst from the AA12. Two loyal Ducci soldiers explode into crimson fog. He squeezed off several more shots randomly to suppress any oncoming fire. A gunman near John tried to draw a pistol. John shot him without hesitation. White made a play to turn but John quick on the trigger fired a shot through White's head. First smoke then blood came from the hole in White's already pale white head, his body dropped like a deflating Thanksgiving Day balloon.

Plaster walls shatter under the heavy fire from the AA12 kicking up a white dust storm. The drum is emptied and so Luis let go, allowing the street sweeper to hang from the strap. His next move was to pull two flash grenades, with the pins stuck to the vest; he tugged and threw one to John who tossed it up the stairway. Luis tossed the other in the direction of the front hall. Both brothers ran at full sprint out of the house through a shower of bullets coming from Logan's men. John shot over his shoulder as they exited, emptying his clip.

John was out first. He dropped his empty rifle and pulled a pistol in time to shoot a soldier right outside the door. As Luis passed the doorway he let go of two fragment grenades, dropping on either side of him. They were already passed the front door when the first two grenades went off. The brother's didn't stop running. They got into the Cadillac, still idling and speed off, laying rubber halfway down the drive. The only thing chasing was random gunfire, then two more explosions.

On the other side of town Marty paced back and forth in front a payphone beside the 7-eleven. Across the street the ocean crashed with curling wave after wave. The tide was high and the moon was full. Behind him Cheryl sat on a motorcycle that had been laid down. She had a backpack around her shoulders and impatience on her face.

"Get to it Marty so we can get the hell out of here already."

"Right." The former Jai Alai player muttered as his shaking hand picked up the receiver. He dropped a couple coins in and punched the buttons. "Ah..Lito please." He is made to wait then, "Yeah I ah sorry to call, I tried to reach Rico but he ain't nowhere to be found. The Solos got your case and they want a meeting."

Incoherent shouts came from the receiver forcing Marty to hold the phone out from his ear. He talked over the shouting. Marty rushed his words, "Ah... Colossal and Grand street. There's a construction site. Ah two or two thirty. Two a.m." and hung up in a hurry.

Everything inside him was numb. His exhale did not seem to end until Cheryl shouted, "Well can we go now?"

Marty would not remember the walk to the motorcycle or putting on the open faced helmet. It was for the best. The distraction of impending death forced Marty into an autopilot that allowed him to start up the motorcycle. The straight pipes drowned out the sound of the ocean.

"Yeah baby we're going, as far away from this town as we can." He steadied himself, twisting back on the throttle.

On the corner of Colossal and Grand was a construction site. Two steel skeletons disappeared somewhere among the stars. A sleek black Hemi Charger growled to a stop. John jumped out and whacked the latch holding the gates together. Luis pulled through and parked his new Dodge in the back of the lot. The corners of each steel skeleton came to a point creating half a diamond the size of a major league infield. Buried among the bobcats and back hoes was the Scout; back up was here and in position. John took out two briefcases, flipped them open and checked the contents of each. He closed them and wiped both cases down.

"Now we sit and wait." John said taking in as much of the dark construction site as possible. His eyes darted from place to place looking for Backup.

Luis stepped out from behind a low stack of cinderblocks. "I picked my spot, you have yours?" He asked making his way towards John.

John looked around for possible cover. Spinning his head in all directions he said, "I'll find a [place when the time is right."

"Always prepared." Luis laughed. Then his face sank. "Listen, I've been thinking about what you said, about leaving."

John looked to the ground moving a tiny mound of earth with his boot. "Yeah."

"You're right. We'll always be gamblers but we don't have to do it here. As soon as we collect on Ducci and Lito we will split this sewer."

John nodded and said getting back to business, "Let's hope Marty was able to get that message to King Lito."

At ten minutes past two, a black sedan followed by a white Rolls Royce pulled slowly into the work site.

152

Men emptied out holding guns and anticipating trouble. The rear window of the Rolls rolled down a quarter way. Smoke billowed out then the tip of a nose and a black mustache peek out. Words were exchanged between the mustache and a man with a gun. Next a hand came out with the digits directing men where to go. One man reported back that there was no activity. Lito remained in the car.

It was not long before two more sedans pulled up to the site from the same entrance as the others. All of Lito's men trained their guns on the cars. Ducci jumped out before most of his men. His eyes were tight and his mouth was pulled to the corners in a grin that expected to be fed.

Both parties expected a set up in one way or another. Each made the decision that they had superior fire power and to walk directly in would ensure a quick victory. Before the two bosses had a chance to speak, the sound of a generator kicking on followed flood lights popping on temporarily blinding those in front.

Luis and John approached from in the light. Each on carried a case.

"I'm glad all of you had the balls to show." John said to the stunned audience.

"What the hell is going on and what's with the cases?" Ducci wanted results. He would be the bull in the china shop until he got them.

"Better question is what is this hood doing here?" Lito said with a jerking thumb towards Ducci.

The Bosses exchanged dirty looks. Ducci never had the respect of Lito. Though they never were directly in competition, King Lito felt the wealth of the mafia behind him outshined anything Ducci could collect on. In Ducci's anger he began to sway, his hand was at his side giggling keys in his pocket. King Lito folded his arms and puffed on his cigar stoking Ducci's fire. Lito eyed the case nervously. The standoff fell silent.

"Lito, my brother and I wanted to return to you the case you hired us to collect for a twenty percent fee."

Ducci was now interested, that was a large collection fee. Doubts of his blinding rage to see The Collectors dead began to dissipate.

Lito began to back pedal, "I never hired you two bums to make a collection. I don't know what you've been smoking but hell no."

"Ducci we told you we would bring you your cousin's killer. Here he is." John pointed to Lito.

Ducci became confused adding to his anger. "This Latin Hood don't want a war with me. He knows I would crush 'em." Ducci spat. It was a way of getting the last of his bloated lie out of his mouth. Everyone present knew Lito's mafia backed soldiers would wipe Ducci off the East Town map.

"Puta Madre," Lito whispered, then shouted, "Fuck you Collectors!" Lito waved a hand to signal his men to fire. POOF. A silenced rifle shot whispered, breaking the stillness of the standoff. A gunman from behind the Bosses let out a grunt and fell from a perched position in the scaffolding of one of the buildings. Everyone paused for a second then Hell opened up. Guns blazed, sulfur filled the air. Everyone ran for cover and picked their targets.

Backup took the brunt of the gun fire. It was too much to return accurate shots. He rolled off the platform. A zip line screamed out and slowed his decent, giving him time to sling the M4 and fire randomly, laying down enough rounds to give the brothers time to take cover.

The collector brothers scrambled across the rutted construction site. John took cover behind a Bobcat while Luis found relief behind a stack of cinderblocks. The bullets came in fast and hot. Sparks follow the ping of every ricocheted lead round connecting with the steal Bobcat.

A free for all ensued as Ducci's crew pumped rounds into Lito's Mafiosos. They picked each other off in rapid succession. Soon the shots were few between. Luis popped up locking onto Ducci who was firing his revolver as fast as he could pull the trigger. His eyes pinched the moment he saw Luis stand from behind the cinderblocks. Simultaneously the two squeezed.

Luis' reaction of closing his eyes as the bullet impacted could not be helped. The force of the thirty-eight pushed hard but Luis did not go down. When he opened his eyes Ducci had turned and forced his large frame to move faster than someone that size should. Luis leveled the forty-five but he did not fire. Ducci took two more steps then dropped in the dirt kicking up dust under his collapse.

There was no time to celebrate. The lead continued to fly. John began taking more than he could handle. Luis had to bail him out. He duel wielded forty-fives and shouted as he ran towards John. John moved back meeting Luis at a pile of steal scaffolding. John reloaded and came up intending to kill. His shot was the last.

Silence.

Sulfur drifted through the streaming light. John and Luis moved cautiously from their cover. Backup was out of his hole and began to roll bodies. He fired once more. Dead men lay everywhere. Everything was still. Then the Rolls Royce moved side to side. John signaled to Luis. They ran over to the car.

Lito was sweating in the back seat. His eyes were wide and he fumbled to reload a nickel plated thirty-two. "Go, go." He shouted, slapping the back of the front seat. Lito looked out to see the Solos drawing near. He lunged over the front seat to shake the driver. Pedro slumped to his right revealing a well place shot through the windshield and into his chest. Lito tried to force himself over the seat. He was too fat.

Lito fired sporadically through the passenger's window. John and Luis did not alter their advance.

Luis pulled open the door. John pointed his forty-five at Lito who was pulling the trigger on an empty pistol.

"You know Lito it didn't have to end like this. You could have just had us collect on Tony from the beginning."

"Hey man it's cool. We can work all this out." Lito said with a smile. His eyes drifted to the seat beside the dead driver.

John followed Lito's wondering eyes. He shook his head disapprovingly. "We just did." He said to the most feared boss in all of East Town. The trigger went back easy as it was the moment John wanted since all this started. Brains splattered.

Luis threw a case by the Rolls and the other he wrapped in Ducci's dead fingers.

John, Luis and Backup gathered in the middle of the site. Luis held out a small plastic case full of chips for Backup as payment.

"Thanks for coming."

Backup waved off the payment, "Sorry friend I don't take plastic. Anyway I needed the break from my day job."

"Right, sorry. John pay the man his due."

John handed over a brick of cash to Backup. "So what exactly is your day job?"

"I teach sixth grade social studies." Backup's face remained still.

"Good for you," John said with a crooked smile. "Kids need a good role model these days."

Luis broke up the chat session. "Let's hit the road brother."

The brother collectors headed off for their Charger while Backup got in his Scout. Two sets of headlights came on as the pair of vehicles exited. One went left while the other right.

From a dark corner of the site, blue and red cop lights circled. A cop car coasted forward into the light. The door of the cop car opened. Officer Hagerty stood holding a receiver. "Dispatch, this is Officer Hagerty. I got a real mess down here at Colossal and Grand Streets. We're gonna need some crime scene investigators and whole lotta body bags."

Bonus Collectors Story:

Just what did John and Luis Solo do for Officer Hagerty?

Officer Darnell Hagerty sat idle in his patrol car. The sun was rising in the east on its way directly over head. It was 84 degrees by ten o'clock in the morning, July in Florida. Car after car sped down A1A, past the indifferent officer. Hagerty was preoccupied. His thoughts were as tied as his hands. He needed someone to help, someone outside the law but could work inside of it.

A red Fox Body Mustang zoomed by slinging around slower moving cars. Hagerty fired up his patrol car but failed to drop it into gear. His thoughts remained tied. Rita, his wife, was sitting at the dinette table crying when he left for work this morning.

A flat black shoe box 1950 Ford Coupe rumbled by at the same speed as the Mustang. This time Hagerty could not sit idle any longer. He flipped on the lights and called in to dispatch he was in pursuit.

Swinging the patrol car south on to A1A he gunned the motor to catch the hot rod. Traffic cruised at a medium pace. The officer had to be careful of all the out-of-state licensed cars; they were the most reckless. Confused by the unfamiliar surroundings, tourists always make the most dramatic attempts at getting out of a cop's way.

The black hotrod cut up Silver Beach headed for the mainland. Beyond the hotrod, Hagerty could make out the Mustang barreling ahead as well.

Together the three speeding Fords neared the bridge at Silver Beach. The Mustang blew the light at Peninsula and hit the steel grated bridge. From the Inner Coastal the tip of a sail could be seen heading north. The lights on red and white striped barricades began to flash as the poles dropped, crossing the street.

A fog horn blew as the Mustang punched all it had out of the exhaust. The black hotrod hung tight but went into a skid as the steel bridge began to lift and separate in the center. The Mustang timed it right and caught the apex with enough speed to clear the gap. The driver of the much heavier antique steel hotrod knew better and Hagerty was glad.

The hotrod was not done though. Burning rubber and laying two black stripes the V-8 powered coupe spun around and charged out off the bridge. Hagerty swung his patrol car sideways and prayed the driver would stop. The driver did with only inches between them.

Letting out a deeply held breath, Hagerty jumped out of his patrol car with a Glock in hand.

"Let me see those hands!"

The black tinted window went down. A pair of Caucasian hands protruded. From the passenger side window a pair of darker, Hispanic hands came. On his wrist was a gold watch.

"Come on out."

The doors popped and out came John and Luis Solo.

John spoke first, "Officer we are Collectors in pursuit of a dept."

Hagerty kept the pistol on them and asked to see some badges.

Carefully John and Luis pulled brass Collectors badges with matching photo id's and handed them over to Hagerty.

The East Town Cop made them wait as he radioed in the badge numbers. Meanwhile John and Luis watched the red Mustang stroll along Beach Street safely on the other side of the river. There went their ten percent cut of seventy-five thousand dollars.

Satisfied with the id's Hagerty holstered his weapon. He handed back the badges and said, "When you saw my lights you should have radioed in who you are and what you were chasing."

The Solo brothers nodded, they knew all the rules of being a legitimate collector in East Town.

Hagerty stared blankly at the brothers with tired eyes. His brain was yelling at his body to write out a ticket to these casino tax collectors, but his hands remained still.

"Officer, if you don't mind we would like to get going."

"Yeah, sure. I'll let you off with a warning." Hagerty walked back to his patrol car.

John looked over to Luis. A look from one brother to the other spelled out volumes. Luis shook his head 'no' but knew it would not stop John.

"Officer," John called as he jogged to catch up with Hagerty, "I don't mean to pry but what's up?" The Solo brothers have had run ins with every cop in East Town. Sometimes even for a job. Many times cops think they can borrow some money and show their relatives a good time at the tables and think they don't have to pay it back. It doesn't work that way. Most of the time, the cops are helping the Solos on collections and it's usually *a don't get in my* way and *I won't get in yours* unsaid agreement. This time John wanted to get in the way.

"You better get after your money." Hagerty said without turning around.

"Come on, I know something's up." John would not give up. Being able to read people was a skill these two brothers were born with. Even strangers could be read. Most people's behavior is predictable in defined circumstances, such as this. Hagerty should have written them a citation or called in back up and dragged them down town. He did neither.

"Look, Mr. Solo, I aint got the time so bug off."

"Officer," John looked to the cop's name tag, "Hagerty. Cops and collectors don't always get along and we don't have to. You have a very defined set of rules to play by to get your man and we have ours. These rules operate on different frequencies but every once in a while they line up. So what gives?"

That clicked with Hagerty. This tall white man in a sweat stained t-shirt and jeans made sense, this is what Hagerty had asked for.

"Okay kid. Pull that beast of a car over to that parking lot and let's chat."

****

The men stood around their cars and discussed the officer's problem. It started back earlier in the year when his wife's brother, Troy, decided to open a night club on International Boulevard. He got the usual permits and borrowed a load of cash from Hagerty to grease the wheels of government for a liquor license. That was Hagerty's retirement.

"Things were going good until Troy decided not to have slots or tables in his club. He called it Local Heroes and wanted it to be a locals-only place, the kind for casino workers to go after work and get away from their jobs."

This did not sound like a place to relax for the Solo brothers but to each his own, they could understand.

"That's when Councilman Harry Twindle made an appearance. He put pressure on Troy to put in slots. When Troy refused, suddenly a health inspector named Stephen showed every week writing new citations and the next thing you knew the liquor license was gone."

"You mean they pulled it?" Luis asked, now glad his brother had chased the officer down.

"Not exactly, it just disappeared. On record and on paper. The actual license is gone. City claims not to know anything about it. City says some kind of filing error on their end and unless he can show the license it doesn't exists. You know how much those damn things cost?" Hagerty sat on the fender of his patrol car with slumped shoulders.

John looked to Luis. Crooked government officials, the best kind of junkie to collect on. Government Officials with dirty hands were an all too regular occurrence in East Town. Something in the water or more likely the green pumping out of casinos was turning their minds to mush and their hearts dark. Collecting on an official of the state was walking a razor's edge for sure. They granted the badge and could take it away, but a good collector had a casino at his back and that always trumped a government card.

Luis spoke up, "We're in."

Hagerty took a second to gather his thoughts, thoughts that had been so singular until now. "But you boys don't know me, I mean there just aint no reason to go getting involved."

"Love it or hate it," Luis began, "this is our town."

John finished his brother's thought, "And every man should know the odds he is playing."

Hagerty extended his black hand to meet with the white and brown hands in agreement.

****

A muggy night awaited the collectors as they stepped out of the Beach Palm Casino and Hotel. Beachside was lit up with the board walk in full swing. A band played at the end of the pier as music of a different kind came from arcades where children learned the rules of games of chance.

Luis called the valet over and ordered his Cadillac to be brought up. John grumbled, preferring to take his vintage steel instead. They had this argument before and in the summer A/C was essential. The 1950 had been retro fitted with new A/C but the Caddy had it in the seats as well.

A few calls found them their health inspector. Stephen Rodney was working tonight. He was planning to visit *Seafarer's*, a restaurant tucked under one of the large concrete cross-river bridges linking the beachside to the mainland.

The Cadillac sat parked under the bridge with the A/C blasting. They gathered a general description of Stephen, balding brown hair, glasses and usually in a short sleeved button down shirt and he always came alone.

"Could that be him?" Luis asked aloud as a man meeting all the descriptors got out of a late model M3 BMW and headed for the restaurant.

"Couldn't be." John thought out loud. Health inspector, balding brown hair, glasses and short sleeve button down was the description. No one mentioned a six foot four inches frame supporting two hundred and thirty pounds of meat.

The brothers got out of the car and went in the restaurant. They were given a table inside next to one of many large bay windows looking out over the river.

The waitress was named Amber and unusually perky for being in her thirties. A trait the brothers knew they could exploit if need be.

Amber took their order of a coke for John and un-sweet iced tea for Luis. They watched as Stephen consulted with the manager on duty and proceeded to walk around taking verbal notes into his cell phone.

The drinks came and so did an appetizer. The brothers stalled on ordering incase Stephen left early.

"I guess you're here for the game." Amber said with a bounce.

"Yep." John said looking to the large TV's. "We love soccer."

"Football." Luis mumbled under his breath.

"Hey Luis who do we have on this game?" John pulled his phone to double check his bets for the day.

"I'm rooting for Bocca, the ones from Argentina." Amber grinned.

"Oh you follow soccer?" Luis asked. "My team is Nacional."

"Yeah. My mother is from Argentina." She said widening her smile and crinkling her blue eyes.

After the silent pause she filled in the gap. "You wouldn't know it right? My grandparents moved there from Germany, after the war." Amber collected the menus and bounced off.

John laughed. "Nazis."

"I don't care, I'm still going after her."

"Nazis man."

Luis shrugged, "They were just building a better race."

"That is so messed up." The pair laughed at their own twisted sense of humor. Just then a commotion came from the kitchen. Luis twitched his head in that direction as John looked.

John pulled his cell phone and switched on the video camera. He zoomed in to watch Stephen get tough with the manager. The restaurant was too loud as the game kicked off and fans began to cheer. John had to get closer.

He headed towards the end of the bar where it met the kitchen. There he stood with his phone out pretending to be texting. He was close enough to catch sound.

"Look at these curly hairs!" Stephen pinched something out of the mashed potatoes. "This place is in serious violation."

"Come on Mr. Rodney. You know those weren't in there." Said the timid manager.

"You calling me some kind of liar? I can shut this place down in a heartbeat." Stephen grumbled within inches of the manager's face. "One week to come up with the money or you're closed."

John looked back at Luis. He slid his index finger across his throat then touched his face causally so as not to attract attention with the death motion.

The pair followed Stephen out to the parking lot catching up to him before he got into his BMW.

"Hey we need to talk to you." Luis called to the inspector.

Stephen came around with a sneer across his squared face. "What?"

John started, "You took something that doesn't belong to you and we are collecting back."

"Who sent you? Doesn't matter punk, I got protection, government protection." Stephen flicked his name badge clipped to the pocket of his button down shirt.

"The liquor license for Local Heroes on International. We want it."

Stephen scoffed. "You clowns couldn't afford it. I told that dude one hundred grand. I'm telling you two hundred."

"Not the hard way." Luis sighed then clobbered the big man with a shot to jaw. He staggered back bracing himself against his car.

Stephen shook his head bringing his senses around. He straightened, and then brought both his large fists up and grin.

Luis danced back luring Stephen away from his car. Once in the open of the parking lot, Luis shot in, pushing the man's right elbow up and wrapping his arms around the man's waist. He planted his foot and tossed the man to the ground. Once on the ground it was easy for Luis to get Stephen in a submission hold.

John stepped up and plucked the inspector's badge from his chest. "We're going after Harry Twindle next." He held the phone up and played back the incriminating video.

Through the straining chokehold Stephen spat, "Okay, okay. I give." He tapped the asphalt. Luis let him up.

The man caught his breath then said, "Look I'll give you what I know on Twindle if you can leave me out of it."

John flipped back over to record. "Go on."

Stephen went on to outline the whole racketeering business he and Councilman Twindle had set up. Stephen listed names and dates of routine cash pick-ups. "I got one tonight behind Club Meteor. The councilman will be there."

****

On the ride over the brothers barley talked about what needed to be done. They did not have to, this stuff was routine for them. Having lived together for the last fifteen years it was easy to move without speaking.

"So the councilman likes extortion."

"Then I say we hit him with blackmail."

Outside Club Meteor a white Prius sat parked with a big City of East Town crest slapped on the side. The councilman wasted every cent of tax payers' dough. He could not be bothered with driving his own car to an illegal racketeering operation.

The white haired man sat behind the wheel. His drooping jowls were illuminated by the light from the playing radio. In the reflection of his glasses the Meteor sign flashed. His boney fingers wrapped around the wheel as John pulled Stephen's BMW near.

John rolled the tinted window down. "Expecting someone else?" he said to the shocked councilman. A face of a woman equally shocked rose from the councilman's lap.

"Councilman Twindle, are we in trouble?" she said with smeared lipstick.

"No. Just sit still." The councilman started to drop his hand towards his fly when John pointed a forty-five at the man.

"Out of the car." John said. When the councilman went for his fly again John said, "Nope. Out."

The old man got out of the car. His face a beet red, filled with viral hate for this punk who apparently did not know who Councilman Twindle was. Little blue and purple veins began to squirm at each temple.

John forced him to stand there with his fly down until Luis pulled up in the Cadillac.

Both collectors stood with folded arms looking down at the frail old man.

"Get on with it." The grey haired man said knowing he was about to be shook down.

"You have something we came to collect." Luis said.

"The liquor license for Local Heroes."

The man began to bark the usual crap he gave to young patrolmen who pulled him over or to maitre d when they made him wait for a table.

In the middle of the man's pathetic rant, John played back the video of Stephen in the restaurant out in the parking lot. The old man quieted down.

"You can't use that in court." He said from the corner of his mouth.

"We don't intend to. You know how viral the web is these days. Give us the license and we're gone."

"I keep them in my office."

The trio took a trip down to city hall. They passed security and went on up to the eighth floor.

The office was surprisingly sparse with a standard wooden desk and overstuffed red leather chair behind it. A single bookcase held large legal books. Harry ran his finger along the spines and stopped at one dealing with maritime law. He opened it and pulled out a manila older. Inside the folder were a half dozen other licenses.

John grabbed them. "What the hell?"

Luis looked over his brother's shoulder as John flipped through them. "You're a real piece of shit Twindle."

The council stood attempting to look defiant but he knew he was defeated.

John plucked the license for Local Heroes. "The rest of these will be returned by the end of the week or we upload." He pushed play. This time the video showed the shocked Councilman and the woman in his lap.

****

Days later Local Heroes was back up and running. John and Luis stopped in for a drink. Hagerty was behind the bar and more than happy to serve them.

"Whatever you're drinking, it's on the house!" Hagerty said as the brothers took a seat.

Hagerty served up a couple of Johny Walkers. "Man you two really came through. My wife's happy, her brother is happy and we have our retirement back up and running."

"That's great Hagerty, but what are you doing behind the bar?"

"It's my day off. I still got to keep an eye on things." Hagerty got serious for a moment when he said, "I know collecting is a tough job. Anything you boys need and I will do it." He laid a hand on the bar then poured another round.

"That day will come Hagerty." John said.

THE COLLECTORS will

return in

THE WRONG BET

More titles from Forker Media can be found at www.forkermedia.com